ARTHUR SCHNITZLER

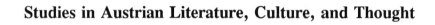

Studies in Austrian Literature, Culture, and Thought

Sol Liptzin

ARTHUR SCHNITZLER

ARIADNE PRESS

Library of Congress Cataloging-in-Publication Data

Liptzin, Solomon. 1901-
    Arthur Schnitzler / by Sol Liptzin
        p.   cm. -- (Studies in Austrian literature, culture, and
    thought)
    Originally published: New York : Prentice-Hall, 1932
    ISBN 1-57241-013-2
    1. Schnitzler, Arthur, 1862-1931--Criticism and interpretation.
    I. Title. II. Series
    PT2638.N5Z832   1994
    833'.8--dc20
                                    94-48728
                                    CIP

Cover design:
Art Director and Designer: George McGinnis

Copyright ©1995
by Ariadne Press
270 Goins Court
Riverside, CA 92507

TO

RICHARD BEER-HOFMANN

Sol Liptzin

TABLE OF CONTENTS

PREFACE

When it was first published in 1932, Sol Liptzin's book on Arthur Schnitzler was welcomed as the first comprehensive examination of the complete works to appear after Schnitzler's death in 1931. Liptzin enjoyed the advantage of knowing Schnitzler personally and, as is apparent throughout his enthusiastic, sympathetic account, greatly admired and respected the Viennese author. The profound empathy with which the book was written shows on every page. However, his admiration by no means influences Liptzin's keen insight and critical judgment which make the work the valuable contribution that it has been and that it remains. Liptzin not only brings a thorough understanding of his subject to his presentation, but he also adds the advantage of writing with flair and fluency. This introductory study, unencumbered by footnotes, engages and holds the reader's interest in the manner of a novel.

Rather than proceeding chronologically, Liptzin has organized the book by major themes. In each chapter he treats a basic human problem confronted by Schnitzler, and analyzes it in the appropriate works, discussing it in the overall context of Schnitzler's life and oeuvre. Liptzin benefitted greatly from the opportunity to utilize the many manuscripts in the literary estate, quite probably the first person to do so, making it possible for him to feature the genesis of various important texts, tracing their evolution sometimes over periods as long as twenty years. This information was totally new at the time and still remains valid.

Beyond all of these other positive qualities, however,

the feature that endows this book with its special appeal and makes it worthy of reprinting after some sixty years, during which so much other scholarship has appeared and been forgotten, is the amazing accuracy of Liptzin's findings. He demonstrates through his critical skill the ability to penetrate to the essence of Schnitzler's writings in a way not often achieved in much longer, more detailed, and fully documented works. His interpretations, proceeding from the genesis of the individual plays and prose works, continue to be as relevant today as his style remains fresh and appealing. For all of these reasons this book is being made available to a new generation of readers both to learn from and to enjoy.

Donald G. Daviau

ARTHUR SCHNITZLER

CHAPTER I

THE DANCE OF DEATH

THE call of death came to Arthur Schnitzler on October 21, 1931, while he was busy revising his drama *The Call of Life*, which was to be performed on the occasion of his seventieth birthday, on May 15, 1932. For years he had lived in semiseclusion and had never given interviews—although after his death several so-called interviews found their way into print. Always frank in answering questions about his literary work, he resented all written references to his personal life. When asked once for complete biographical data, he submitted the following: "I was born in 1862 and was a physician." Since his death various legends about him have appeared and will continue to appear. These should be examined with minute care and considerable skepticism. Until the publication, decades hence, of his autobiography and of his diaries, his works form the best record of his life and his personality.

The present study attempts to treat Schnitzler as the thinker and the artist—as the thinker, by tracing the basic ideas embedded in his novels and dramas; as the artist, by tracing the genesis of characteristic works from the first concept until the final, perfected version.

Schnitzler was of Jewish stock. His father, Professor

Johann Schnitzler, was a Viennese throat specialist, who numbered among his patients Adolf Sonnenthal, Charlotte Wolter, and other famous dramatic and operatic stars. Constant association with these theatrical figures stimulated young Arthur to begin the writing of plays while he was still in his boyhood. At first he intended to follow his father's profession. He attended the University of Vienna from 1879 to 1885, and in the latter year he received the degree of doctor of medicine. After three years of practice in various hospitals of Vienna, he joined his father's clinic as an assistant. Meanwhile, in 1886, he began writing medical reviews for the *Wiener Medizinische Presse*, a journal rounded by his father in 1860. In December, 1887, he became editor of the *Internationale klinische Rundschau*, a position that he retained until September, 1894. The articles that bear his signature deal mainly with hypnotism, neurasthenia, telepathy, and psychotherapy. He discusses in detail the works of Krafft-Ebing on sex, and of Lombroso on genius. He praises Sigmund Freud, whose translation of Charcot he calls masterful. Freud later stated that Schnitzler's poetic intuition led to some of the same discoveries as his own researches.

Schnitzler's first non-scholarly publications appeared at the close of the 1880's in Viennese periodicals. Some of his poems and tales are signed "Anatol," a name that he soon selected for the hero of his first playlets. In the fall of 1892 these playlets appeared in book form, with a famous introductory poem by Hugo von Hofmannsthal, who then still bore the pseudonymn "Loris." In 1894 Schnitzler's first full-length play, *Das Märchen*, was presented in Vienna and proved a theatrical failure. This failure was more than compensated for, however, by the success of *Liebelei* during the following year, when it was performed at the Burgtheater under the auspices of the new director, Max Burckhard. Thereafter Schnitzler devoted himself almost entirely to a literary career, producing important dramas and narratives in rapid succession. Most of these are to be found in the eleven volumes of his collected works. Like other poets, Schnitzler could not avoid mirroring himself in his figures. The heroes of whom he was fondest included Stefan von Sala, in *Der einsame Weg*; Heinrich Bermann, in *Der Weg ins Freie*; and Sylvester Thorn, in *Der Gang zum Weiher*. In them we may look for his nearest approach to self-portraiture.

At the turn of the century, Schnitzler, together with Hermann Bahr, Richard Beer-Hofmann, and Hugo von Hofmannsthal, formed the center of a literary movement known as "Young Vienna," a movement that stood in violent opposition to the Naturalism of Berlin and Munich as well as to the pseudo-Classicism of Grillparzer and his epigones. This group dominated Austrian letters until the outbreak of the World War and the rise of Expressionism.

Schnitzler's creative work is largely an expression of his yearning for life and his preoccupation with death. His brooding, melancholy temperament, his extreme sense of moral responsibility, and his social position as a member of a very respectable Jewish, upper middle-class family prevented him from lightly experiencing the frivolities of youth and love. Hence, there arose his subconscious admiration for the magic world in which characters such as Anatol, or Fritz Lobheimer, or Max von Reisenberg flitted about—a world of spring and color and adventure, a world in which he himself was never quite at home. The roots of Schnitzler's personality are to be sought elsewhere, perhaps in that soil which produced figures such as Stefan von Sala and Heinrich Bermann, Falkenir and Sylvester Thorn—sentimental skeptics and ironical idealists, well-mannered heroes who see in all human struggles and ambitions merely the play of marionettes against a background of death.

Schnitzler at his best is not a cheerful poet. Death ever lurks behind the merry words and the light loves of his figures, and often it breaks in unexpectedly upon the gayest feasts. Repeatedly we are reminded that all acts and relations, all eternal vows and far-flung ambitions are but transitory, and that they are destined to be nipped before long. It is this consciousness of death's omnipresence which often lends to Schnitzler's works the peculiar pathos and aroma which we associate with his name. It seems almost as though death exercised a peculiar fascination over him, and he sought to rob it of its fabled terrors by constantly invoking it. Now it appears to him as a lowering of veils over a person and now as an ending to a dialogue. "Is there any intelligent human being," asks his hero, Sala, in *Der einsame Weg*, "who in happy hours thinks in the depths of his soul of anything else save death?"

Only unintelligent people, Schnitzler holds, can speak lightly of life's end. Only those who do not know the full import of being can pass from it without a shudder of horror at its loss. For, the more fully one has tasted of every moment, the more keenly does he feel the bitterness of the final hour of parting from light. The poet Filippo Loschi, in *Der Schleier der Beatrice*, seeks to explain to the "unproblematic" heroine the contrast between life and death: "Your beautiful body, which I now hold in my embrace and through which hot blood pulsates, will soon be merely a thing, even less than a stone. For a stone remains what it is, if I throw it down. You, however, now fragrant and trembling, a source of intense desire and tingling sensation to all who see you, will become an object of horror, an object evoking disgust on the morrow and danger on the day after tomorrow, an object to be buried next to other rotting bodies in order to protect the living. And I myself, even I would shudder at the thought of holding your breathless self in my arms, though your hair and clothes may still be fragrant."

Beatrice comes to Filippo Loschi in order to die a common death with him, since they can no longer live together. But at the critical moment she is overwhelmed by the grim seriousness of the experience and rushes forth from him with the cry of "Life!" upon her lips. Marie Moser, in *Der Ruf des Lebens*, feels that death alone can wipe out her guilt and disgrace; but when the sun comes up, the yearning for its warm rays reasserts itself and she is grateful for each additional breath granted her. When the sweetheart of Felix, in the tale *Sterben*, learns that his days are numbered and that within a year he will have left the ranks of mortals, she is certain that she will not want to survive him. In her intense grief she assures him that she is ready even to take the final step with him. The nearer the terrible day approaches, however, the stronger is the urge of life within her; and, when in his last hour he tries to drag her down with him to the grave, she frees herself from his grasp and with a cry of relief enters into her new span of life.

Schnitzler mistrusts big words, such as "heroism" or "courage," in the face of doom. He feels that no person gladly stakes his life so long as he has reason to love it. If, on the other hand, he stakes it without loving it, why should such an act be regarded as heroic, or even courageous? The veteran Plank, in *Der junge Medardus*, tells his patriotic Austrian comrades, who are carousing before leaving for the front to fight Napoleon, that all their merriment and all their enthusiasm are at bottom merely sublimated fear— hellish fear. The father of Marie Moser, when sent to the battlefront in charge of a squadron, is seized with an indescribable terror while he is waiting for the attack to begin; and it suddenly occurs to him that all this talk of honor and fatherland is pure humbug. What reward, or what gratitude, can warm the dead? He envisages himself thrown with thousands of others into a grave; earth will be piled upon him, and all will be over. There wells up in him an irresistible desire for life, for a home, for a wife and children; and he flees from the battlefield blindly, madly. Similarly, when Lieutenant Albrecht, in the same play, is told that on the morrow he is to die for the greater glory of his fatherland, he replies: "Oh, these are words—words! Nevermore to gallop over a field at dawn with a brightening heaven above you, nevermore to hang on blossoming lips with the fragrance of trembling breasts wafted about you, nevermore for you the sound of a living voice nor the sparkle of sunlight and starlight . . . to sink and bleed away, to end and be buried for all time—if this doesn't make you shudder, my friend, then you understand neither death nor life." Moreover, when Albrecht is reminded that the supreme sacrifice is necessary as an example for those who are to come after us, he still remains sceptical: "After us? Nothing comes after us. The collapse of the sun millions of years hence sounds as loudly in our ears as the funeral speech of the field chaplain at our grave. Nothing comes after us. Our own murderer, even while digging his dagger into our hearts, dies with us. "

Schnitzler himself specifies in the codicil to his will, dated April 29, 1912, that, after his death, absolutely no one is to wear mourning for him. He forbids funeral orations and elaborate funeral rituals. Like Albrecht, he feels that no amount of oratory or weeping can warm the dead, and that the living should not succumb to gloom because of those who have passed on.

Albrecht is but one of the many figures who recur in the dramas and novels of Schnitzler and whom we may designate as *morituri*. They are men and women upon whose foreheads the stamp of death is visible, but who still manage to breathe among the living. Upon them the author lavishes much of his love and his art. These figures, whose final hour is definitely known, regard the daily interests of others as petty and foolish. Against a background of eternity, all words and acts lose much of their glory and importance. The dying journalist, Rademacher, in *Die letzten Masken*, asks the physician at the hospital to call his former friend, the successful author, Weihgast, to his bedside. It is Rademacher's intention to relieve his embittered emotions by lashing this proud person with the most venomous words at his command. He even rehearses his tirade before Weihgast's arrival. But when the two face each other, the journalist's anger gives way to supreme indifference. He feels that he has nothing in common with the joys and sorrows of this man, who will still be alive on the following day. He feels that the dying and the living do not speak the same language, and that there is little they can communicate to each other.

The first of the *morituri* to be depicted by Schnitzler is

Felix, the hero of the tale *Sterben* (1892). In the full flush of youth and amidst the delights of love, Felix is told that he has but one more year to live. At first he tries to laugh off the shadows of fear that creep into his heart. But soon he feels himself utterly defenseless against their menacing blackness. His whole being is concentrated on the one inescapable thought. His every day appears to him a horrible respite, filled with tortures more intense than death itself could devise. He regards himself as a prisoner waiting to be led to the block upon the arrival of the executioner. He begins to hate the people who walk about, because these people will still walk and laugh and weep when he is lying cold and motionless. He abandons all pretense of facing the end without flinching. "To scorn life when one is as healthy as a god, to look stoically into the eye of death when one travels on a vacation in Italy and everything blooms in the brightest colors—that I call simply a pose. Now, take such a gentleman and lock him up in a room; condemn him to fever and let him gasp for breath; tell him that he'll be buried between the first of January and the first of February in the following year; and then let him philosophize to you." The equanimity of Socrates as he drinks the hemlock is, to Felix, merely a pose. The captured rebel who smilingly faces a firing squad is, in the eyes of Felix, a hypocrite. The convict who walks steadfastly to the gallows is but acting a role. All of them are simply attempting to hide the natural fear of death which is gnawing away at their hearts. As a bulwark against this fear, Felix wants to take with him to the grave the person whom he holds dearest. With subtle art, Schnitzler sketches the gradual moral decay of Felix under the influence of his uncontrollable anguish. When his sweetheart, Marie, first tells him that she intends to die with him, he upbraids her for wanting to throw away the most precious gift she possesses—life; and he refuses to accept her sacrifice. As months pass and he grows ever weaker, however, he begins to remind her of her promise and to insist that she fulfill it. But the more he dwells upon this subject, the less attractive does he become to her. The hand of death seems to remove him further and further from her. As he sees her drifting from him, he attempts, with fast-ebbing strength, to strangle her, in order that he will not have to face the unknown alone. She barely escapes, and life is all the sweeter to her thereafter.

Two years after the publication of *Sterben*, Schnitzler depicts another hero under the shadow of death, in the tragedy *Liebelei* (1894). Fritz Lobheimer, who resembles Felix in many ways, is in the midst of a flirtation with Christine, when a gentleman in black rings the bell and asks to be admitted. He is the husband of a woman with whom Fritz had previously carried on an affair. He is the symbol of death. From the moment the stranger enters, we know that Fritz is doomed. For two acts the latter continues his flirting with Christine, but his jests now seem to emanate from a fleshless skull. A searing breath has passed over him and purged him of illusions. Now he can envisage his situation clearly. Now he knows that in Christine's love he might have found lasting happiness—a love that he treated so flippantly in former moments when death was but a vague possibility in a remote future. His upbringing and his social position compel him to engage in a duel with the outraged husband. In obedience to custom, he must let himself be shot for a woman in whom he no longer has the slightest interest. He must leave the world at a moment when its finest joys are just beginning to ripen. At the behest of an outworn convention, he must lay down his life; and he does so unquestioningly.

But his creator, Schnitzler, begins to question. Is not society wrong in demanding, as it has at certain times in the Vienna of the past century, that, in a duel, a person such as Fritz submit himself to his opponent's pistol? By answering the so-called "call of honor," Fritz not only dooms himself, but also brings ruin upon the lives of Christine and her father. Is this show of courage on the part of Fritz necessary, desirable, or justified? How would a person who had once been in the grip of death and who had unexpectedly been restored to health, react to such a situation? Would he, too, feel that the satisfaction of certain conventional requirements was sufficient cause for throwing away one's life? Schnitzler selects such a person as the hero of *Freiwild* (1894), the play written immediately after *Liebelei* and intended as a polemic against the custom of dueling.

Paul Rönning, in Freiwild, is a much nobler character than his predecessors—Anatol, Felix, or Fritz—probably because he once stood on the borderline between life and death and, during his experience there, gained insight concealed from those of unbroken robust health. When asked by his friend, Wellner, why he has lost all desire for work, he replies: "My dear friend, if you were to lie for weeks, as I did, waiting for the end, and were then to recover, as I did, you would see, thereafter, whether you felt anything else except the bliss of breathing again, of belonging to all that grows and blossoms, of speaking again, as others do, of coming days. I want nothing else but to live. This feeling of being alive suffices me."

When Paul is deliberately insulted by Lieutenant Karinski, he retaliates by slapping the officer's face, and he then feels that this action ends the affair. He sees no reason why he should agree to a duel, in which he is likely to be shot. He can understand a person's exposing himself to danger and death for some holy conviction or some vital ideal; but, in so far as he personally is concerned, he places considerable value upon his own existence and does not wish to endanger his life just to satisfy an absurd convention. From that moment, however, he places himself beyond the pale of society and dooms himself to certain disgrace and sudden death. His end is inevitable. It alone proves beyond doubt that his refusal to accept his opponent's challenge is the result, not of cowardice, but of a deep-rooted antagonism to dueling as a test of right and wrong.

In *Das Vermächtnis* (1897), the drama published a year after *Freiwild*, Schnitzler stresses the moral effect upon the living and the dying of death's shadow hovering over them. The dramatist presents an upper middle-class family gathered at the bedside of one of its members who is soon to die. Hugo, the son of Professor Losatti, has been thrown from a horse and suspects that he may not survive his injuries. While in the best of health, he carefully concealed from his respectable parents that he had a mistress and an illegitimate child. But now that his final hour is approaching, he casts from himself his false pride and the fear of social ostracism. He asks his family to fetch his mistress and child, and to care for them as though he had been lawfully married. His request is granted. As long as the family is still under the spell of his death, his wish is faithfully carried out. When, however, weeks pass and the memory of the terrible hour grows dim, then conventional considerations reassert themselves. For a time Hugo's mistress is tolerated because she is the mother of his child. After the death of the child, however, she begins to be regarded as an intruder who no longer has any claim upon the family. When she becomes conscious of her lonely and precarious position, she concludes that her life is no longer worthwhile. Her existence becomes a weary burden to her, and she goes away to commit suicide. Only then does the family realize the unmorality of its attitude. Only then are its social prejudices overcome.

The presence of death, thus, levels all class distinctions. It sweeps away all illusions, all hopes, and all filth. It makes us as pure as children. It gives us strength to live truthfully, in accordance with the laws of our personality rather than in accordance with the dictates of a dominant religious or social philosophy.

In Schnitzler's works the call of life is most alluring as one faces the final hour before death. His human beings then seek to experience the fast-fleeting moments so wholeheartedly that nothing is left for future hours. In *Der Schleier der Beatrice* (1899), the Duke of Bologna, who fears that his town will be sacked on the morrow by the cruel Borgia, proclaims that the final evening is to be given over to Bacchic orgies rather than to fasting and prayer. In *Der Ruf des Lebens* (1905) Lieutenant Max, who must shoot himself before dawn, spends his last hours in the arms of Marie. Katherine, who knows that she is about to die, drinks madly of the most intense sensations, in order to take an abundance of memories with her to the sepulcher. In *Die Hirtenflöte* (1911), the rebellious rabble arrives before the dark walls of a mighty fortress. Nobody is sure of the morrow. Suddenly, out of the silence of the night, there resound shrill laughter, mad cries, stifled moans, woeful howling, and again—laughter. Men and women are taking refuge from fear in one another's arms. "Each seized the person nearest to him, nobody offered resistance, for all knew at once that on the following day everything would be over." In the narrative *Spiel im Morgengrauen* (1926), Lieutenant Willi, who feels that he is morally bound to put an end to his life because he cannot pay his gambling debts, decides to devote his remaining few hours to pleasures of all kinds. He visits the finest restaurant, partakes of the best wine and cigars, and assumes that now he may indulge in anything he pleases.

The bitterest torture that Duke Lionardo, in *Der Schleier der Beatrice* (1899), can devise for the traitor Mariscotti, is to liberate him from his dungeon; to lead him into the resplendent garden, as though his lot had changed for the better; and then, amidst the general merriment, to bind him to a tree. "Let laughter and the sighs of wild lust resound about him; let his glances sink into the luscious, tangled skein of intoxicated bodies; let joys, such as men of his type understand, dance about him in the glare of this red night so that mad desires will eat into his chained and paralyzed limbs. But you, Guidotti, place yourself near him, with drawn dagger, and wait until you receive the command to hurl his head upon the morning dew that will blanket the trodden grass."

Heinrich Bermann, in *Der Weg ins Freie* (1907), plans a libretto which is to center about a person who, because he attempted to assassinate the king, is under sentence of death. The sentence is not executed immediately. Instead of being led to his death, he is brought on board the royal yacht; his chains are removed; he finds himself in the finest society. All bow before him and greet him as though he were a prince. He believes himself saved and participates in the pleasures he finds about him. A stranger approaches him while he is dancing, and tells him that the yacht is sailing to an unknown destination. In days—or weeks—or even months, it will arrive at an island on which he will be killed. His murderer is with him on the yacht. But no one will tell him who he is; and, under penalty of immediate execution, he must not ask. The condemned person regards each day of life as a day of grace and experiences it intensely, splendidly. When the ship reaches land, he prepares for death. Just then the king appears on board and informs him that his sentence has been lifted and that he is again restored to life. He refuses to accept the royal pardon. His existence during the preceding months has had a heightened meaning only because death has been so near and so certain. All the bliss he has experienced has been so precious only because the end might have come at any moment. Now, however, his entire experience has been desecrated for him. His last journey has turned out to be merely an excursion party similar to a thousand other parties. To prevent his last months from becoming a mockery, he hurls himself into the sea.

We are all in the position of the condemned person. We are all marked men. The sentence of death has been pronounced upon each of us at birth, and our final hour is constantly drawing nearer. It is lurking behind us. It may be upon us tomorrow. It may be warded off for a few decades, but it is inescapable. How shall we, to whom this knowledge has been given, fashion the structure of our lives? Shall we continue to forge ambitious plans that require time for completion? Shall we submit to present aches and anxieties for the sake of future joys that may never materialize? Shall we strive for fame, or wealth, or power; or shall we forego all striving and say, as does Georg, the puppet player, in *Der Puppenspieler* (1902): "Fame?—ten years—a thousand years—ten thousand? Tell me in which year immortality begins, and I will trouble myself about fame. Wealth?—ten guilders—a thousand—a million? Tell me how much the world can be bought for, and I will labor for wealth. At present, the difference between poverty and riches, between oblivion and fame is so slight that it is hardly worth my lifting a finger for it."

Perhaps it might be better to experience each fleeting moment fully and intensely, as though it were our last—to embrace it shudderingly and ecstatically with the whole fiber of our personality, as though its successor were never in sight.

Such is the view held by the dazzling, fascinating artist, Julian Fichtner, in *Der einsame Weg* (1903), who, unsobered by moral scruples, floated on through life, up to a certain age, in a continuous intoxication of tenderness, passion, and power. Such is the view of Max von Reisenberg, in *Komödie der Verführung* (1924), whom his friends liken to a caressing spring wind, or to a butterfly that sips at the chalices of flowers—a person who has no definite calling, but whose presence, nevertheless, adds a certain aroma, charm, and friendliness to the bleakest atmosphere. Such, also, is the view of Anatol and Casanova; of Theodor Kaiser, in *Liebelei* (1894); of Filippo Loschi, in *Der Schleier der Beatrice* (1899); of Friedrich Hofreiter, in *Das weite Land* (1910); and of Sylvester Thorn, in *Der Gang zum Weiher* (1926). This view is also shared by Schnitzler's women— from the sweet girls who cluster about Anatol to the more mature heroines of the dramatist's last period. His characters have little faith in a hereafter. At least, they know nothing about it. The question occupying their minds is how to make the most of ever dwindling days on earth—how, with the minimum of effort and psychic expense, to drain every hour of all it can possibly offer.

CHAPTER II

THE LURE OF LOVE

THROUGHOUT the past few decades, the cry of social service has been on everyone's lips. The virtue of continually sacrificing oneself has been preached from schoolroom, pulpit, and press alike, by reactionaries and radicals, by mystics and communists, by Realists, Romanticists, and Expressionists. Patriots have exalted the State as a fetish and have called upon everybody to submit to suffering and death for its sake. The religious revival, resulting from the breakdown of the nineteenth century's absolute faith in the natural sciences, has increased the pressure upon the individual to subordinate his desires and interests to some indefinite good that is beyond rational probing. Leninism, in the name of the proletarian mass, and Fordism, in the name of efficiency, have demanded the whittling down of the range of human idiosyncrasies. Against this anti-individualistic tendency, against this ever rising cry of service and sacrifice, Schnitzler has lifted a voice of protest and condemnation. He has insisted that a healthy organism can be built up only by healthy cells—that a happy society can be based only upon happy beings. The first aim of every being ought, therefore, to be the expression of his ego and the promotion of his personal happiness. "It is one's right," says Sala, in *Der einsame Weg*, "to live one's life fully, with all the ecstasy and all the shudders that may lie concealed therein." Those who preach the necessity of martyrdom, Schnitzler counters with the assertion that martyrdom has always been a proof of the intensity of one's faith—not the correctness of that faith. The martyr does not compel others to believe as he does; at best, he compels them to believe in his capacity for sacrifice.

Schnitzler never tires of stressing that the joy of life ought to be the primary concern of each individual. Filippo Loschi, in *Der Schleier der Beatrice*, regards as a grand illusion the commonly accepted belief that we should not forsake our friend, or wife, or country, even though each means nothing to us. To him there is only one truth, joy—no matter whence it comes. The physician in *Der Ruf des Lebens* impresses upon the heroine, Marie, that the most horrible words which can ever ring in her ears are the words "too late," and warns her that the duty she owes to herself is more important than any duties she may owe to others. The hours go by and never return. Yet, of each hour we retain a certain taste and aroma that we remember forever. Leo Mildner, in *Märchen*, holds that experience—no matter what pangs may seem to accompany it—is essentially synonymous with joy. "Everything that is life and movement, everything that stirs up the soul, is a bit of joy." Youth, above all, should enter upon life as he might come into a wonderful garden with intertwining roads. Young people must be eager to breathe in its fragrance and to pluck its ripening fruits. "As long as one is young," says the wise Sala, "all doors are open; and, before every door, the world begins."

Schnitzler's first symbol of youth is Anatol; and, though he treats this character with increasing irony, he cannot conceal a certain admiration for him. Anatol may be full of faults, but he is also full of glamor and wit. He may be inconstant, but he also possesses the magic gift of genuinely and repeatedly falling in love for the first time. He may be sentimental, but his sentimentality is preferable to the cynicism of his companion.

Anatol is the aesthetic epicurean. He can sketch a little. He can play the piano fairly well. He even writes occasional verses. He appears frivolous simply because he tries to avoid troublesome cares. He appears faithless only because he is so faithful to every new experience that he does not wish to be burdened with the yoke of every former experience. He has no definite calling. He has no family; and, even if he had one, he would not take his responsibilities too seriously. His prime object in life is the pursuit of women. If upbraided for not engaging in a more useful vocation, he would reply that he could not picture a more useful occupation than that of increasing the measure of joy in this earthly vale of tears. The finest joys, he holds, are those which are daintily sipped and not those which are rudely gulped. He is least melancholy when he merely nips at wine, and love, and beauty. The sky must not be too blue. The flowers must not be too fragrant. The birds must not sing too lustily. The sweet maidens must not be too passionate. Perfect poise and ease must be maintained under all circumstances. No matter what the provocation, one ought never to be swept off his feet. He ought to meander among many adventures, but he ought not to hurl himself rashly upon any one single path after he has boldly burned all his bridges behind him. One ought to be able to extract a certain delight even from sadness; and strong joy is best assimilated when sweetened by a bit of tempered melancholy.

The "Anatol" mood is best expressed in the one-act plays which appeared in 1889 and 1890 under the title of this principal character, and which first brought Schnitzler to the attention of a wider reading public. Somewhat earlier, the young author had already used the name "Anatol" as his own pseudonymn, when he published his youthful poems in the Viennese periodical *An der schönen blauen Donau.* The very titles of these poems, such as "Lieder eines Nervösen" or "Der Blasierte," suggest an atmosphere of "over-sophistication." Their most prominent theme, light-hearted love in its subtle variations, is, however, more fully developed in the "Anatol" scenes, seven of which Schnitzler included in his collected works.

In these scenes the dramatist depicts, with charming wit and delicate humor, the graceful philandering of his frivolous and melancholy hero. "Frivolous and melancholy" may impress one as an apparent contradiction; but, to Schnitzler, the former is a necessary corollary of the latter. Frivolity is the easiest escape from the sad contemplation of the flight of time. Anatol would like to experience much. He hungers for the fruits of life. He would agree with Sala that we probably have the right to do whatever we wish to do. He would agree, furthermore, that, perhaps, it may even be our duty to perform every good deed and every piece of villainy that lie within the scope of our capacity for experience. But alas, laws and social conventions hem us in. It is so unpleasant to outrage public opinion. It is so inconvenient to endanger our reputation. It is so uncomfortable to be a real hero, or a real rogue. But, suppose we were to turn our back upon the "great world" of wrestling ambitions and conflicting wills, and to betake ourself to the "little world" of amours. There, if we were graced with excellent manners, a charming personality, sufficient leisure, considerable income, and fine social position, we could play a dominating role. We could go through "bitter-sweet" crises, victories, and defeats, without ever putting up a very considerable stake.

In *Weihnachtseinkäufe*, Anatol draws a picture of this "little world" in which he is most at home. "Imagine a little, dusk-lit room—so small—with painted walls—and even then, still too bright. A few cheap old prints, with faded titles, hang here and there. A dangling lamp, covered with a shade. From the window at twilight, the view over gradually disappearing roofs and chimneys . . . and when spring comes, the garden on the opposite side will bloom and be fragrant."

The heroine of this world is the "sweet" girl, a literary type created by Schnitzler. She is not very elegant, nor unduly intelligent, nor fascinatingly beautiful. But she is always pleasant, and always free from care. She generally lives alone. She has no father and no mother—not even an aunt. She receives the first kiss with a smile and the last one with very tender regret. She is never the cause of tragic complications, although her feelings are genuine and she loves with her whole dainty little heart. Today she may wait for Anatol. If he comes, she will laugh with him, and she will caress and flutter about him. If he fails to appear, she will weep a moment, and then find comfort in the arms of his successor.

This dreamlike world loses all its magic at the slightest touch of skepticism. Max is Schnitzler's symbol for the skeptic. The many beautiful colors woven by illusion are rent by the merciless hand of this logician. When Anatol succeeds in hypnotizing Cora, whose faithfulness he doubts and when he succeeds in getting her to answer all his questions truthfully, then Max urges him to ask the momentous question as to whether or not she has remained faithful. But Anatol refuses. He prefers to remain in ignorance of the answer. If her pretended faithfulness, or her oft-avowed love, is but an illusion, he prefers to treasure that illusion as long as possible—a point of view which the practical realist, Max, cannot endorse. Not that Max disdains the love of a Cora or a Bianca! But he does not wax sentimental over it. For him no atmospheric veil is necessary to cover reality in order to render it more attractive or palatable. Anatol and Max are not merely creations of a momentary whim of the author. They have their roots deep in his personality. This is apparent from the fact that they recur under different names in many of Schnitzler's works. Up to a certain point we may discern in Anatol, the artist, and in Max, the scientist; in Anatol, the poet, and in Max, the physician; in Anatol, the personification of his creator's dreams, wishes, and longings, and in Max, the symbol of the active, responsible, skeptical being. These opposite, yet complementary, types grow older with Schnitzler. They change form and climb, but they rarely leave him. They point to a dualism in his nature. They represent the two poles of his personality. Through these types he often expresses his deepest feelings and wisest thoughts, as, for example, in the dialogues between Julian Fichtner and Marquis von Sala, in *Der einsame Weg;* or between Friedrich Hofreiter and Director Aigner, in *Das weite Land*; or between Sylvester Thorn and Freiherr von Mayenau, in *Der Gang zum Weiher.*

In Schnitzler's early works these dialogues center about women. In the Anatol playlets, woman is treated frivolously. She is seen through the eyes of philandering young men to whom she is merely a source of adventure and pleasure—a being to be looked down upon with a mocking smile—a plaything to be entertained with kisses, caresses, and honeyed words. In *Märchen* (1891) and in *Liebelei* (1894),

Schnitzler presents the game of love as it is viewed by woman. Then it assumes a more serious aspect. What may be merely a gay flirtation for the man is often a much more serious concern for the girl. It is love, life—everything. It is laden with deepest tragedy.

When Christine, the heroine of *Liebelei*, is tempted by Fritz, the charming and brilliant young man, she flares up in love and is ready to give him her body and soul, her youth and fair name. He, however, seeks in her merely a pleasant recreation for idle hours. In her arms he wants to recover from an exciting and dangerous affair that he has had with a married woman. He is interrupted in this pastime by the husband of his former mistress, who insists upon retaliation. The evening before the duel is pleasantly spent by Fritz at the home of Christine. He does not let her suspect that a perilous experience awaits him on the morrow, lest the knowledge disturb the sweet atmosphere associated with her. On the following morning Fritz is shot. It is not until after his burial that Christine finds out from his friend, Theodor, about the duel. To her horror she learns that, just at the time when he meant everything to her, he sacrificed his life for another woman. Frantically she inquires of Theodor whether or not Fritz left some message or letter for her. To calm her, Theodor tells her that Fritz spoke of her, also, on the final, fateful morning. "Of me, too, he spoke! Of me, too! And of what else? Of how many other people—of how many other things that meant just as much to him as I? Of me, too! Oh, God! . . . And of his father, and of his mother, and of his friends, and of his room, and of spring, and of the city, and of everything else that was somehow connected with his life and that he had to leave, just like me . . . of all this he spoke to you, and of me, as well . . . "I am sure he loved you," interposes Theodor. "Love! He? I was nothing more for him than a pastime—and he died for another woman! And I—I adored him! Didn't he know it? . . . That I gave him everything I could give him—that I would have died for him—that he was my God and my heaven? Didn't he notice it? How could he go away from me with a smile—go away from this room, and let himself be shot down for somebody else?"

Christine is broken by the experience which for Fritz, the man, was hardly more than a light-hearted adventure. Even if she were to survive the blow, her whole future would be marred. Puritanical society—the same society that tolerantly shrugs its shoulders at the escapades of a Fritz or an Anatol—would look upon her as a fallen woman. This attitude Schnitzler has violently attacked in his drama *Märchen*, which was completed in 1891, three years before *Liebelei*.

Fanny, the heroine of *Märchen*, has twice loved with all the sincerity and ardor of youth, and has twice been disappointed in the objects of her affection. Just when she is beginning to lose her moral hold upon herself, she meets Fedor Denner, a poet and idealist, whose words sound to her like the words of a savior. Fedor, proud of his modern views, openly protests against the double standard of morality, and he vigorously maintains that men are wrong in despising women who have erred and in regarding them as fallen creatures who deserve no trust nor forgiveness. When Fanny, the girl he loves, hears him proclaim these ideas, she bends down to him and kisses his hand—a mute confession that she, too, has a past. Faced with the application of his liberal doctrines to his own specific case, Fedor is compelled to acknowledge defeat. In theory he may agree that the woman who gives herself to a man because of pure love, and with no thought of the consequences, probably acts more morally than one who does not love and marries simply for a home and comfort. In practice, however, Fedor finds himself damning the former and condoning the offense of the latter. To his dismay, he discovers that he is not really big enough to forgive and to forget. "There is no kiss chaste enough, no embrace glowing enough, and no love lasting enough to efface old kisses and former love."

Fedor begins with an attack on the double standard of morality on the basis of logic and ends with a defense of the double standard on the basis of male psychology. In spite of his fine-spun words, his attitude is not radically different from that of Schnitzler's other heroes, who, in their youth, regard love purely as a fascinating game in which the rules have been laid down by man. This game has phases that are comic and deceptive, tender and coarse, passionate and treacherous. In it man risks little, while woman stakes her all. Anatol, who is a master-hand at this game, takes his own faithlessness for granted, but he is harsh toward Emilie because of her past. Filippo Loschi, in *Der Schleier der Beatrice*, thinks it is perfectly proper for him to desert his betrothed, Teresina, when she needs him most; but he drives Beatrice from him in scorn because she dares to dream of another man. Julian Fichtner, in *Der einsame Weg*, does not scruple to lead his friend's fiancée astray, and to abandon her after giving her a child; but he cannot pardon Irene Herms a slight indiscretion, though she humbles herself in the dust before him. When he meets her decades later and she explains to him that, after all, her transgression was not so very serious, he replies merely: "Not so serious? You may be right. But, if it strikes one of us, it does make him rather angry. And, even if we had become reconciled, it would never have been the same thereafter. "

The problem of faithfulness and faithlessness in the relation between the sexes has too often been regarded solely from the viewpoint of the man, and it has too long been solved by dogmatic formulae based on inherited moral and religious prejudices rather than by a careful examination of the psychic factors involved. Who can say whether, in certain instances, unfulfilled wishes are not more destructive to human happiness than crassest infidelity might be? Who can demark the line at which unfaithfulness begins? Is it with an illicit act, a wayward thought, or a mere longing?

Der Schleier der Beatrice is young Schnitzler's most ambitious attempt to answer these questions—his boldest effort to destroy the misconceptions that obscure a fair judgment of woman.

Originating in a pantomime of 1892, entitled *Der Schleier der Pierette*—a pantomime which Schnitzler did not consider worth publishing—the drama underwent several transformations before reaching its final form. At first the author intended the action to take place in Vienna at the beginning of the nineteenth century. The leading character is a retired young officer, Hans von Traun, who has fallen into evil ways and is drowning his disgust with life in wine and women. This hero has many of the traits that are later attributed to the poet Filippo Loschi. He makes the acquaintance of Agathe Jörger, later renamed Beatrice Nardi, a young girl all athirst with desire for love. For a while they live together in sensual, passionate joy, but finally they have to part. She must marry a rich merchant. She promises, however, that if she cannot reconcile herself to the mate who has been forced upon her, she will return to Hans, in order to die with him. He is convinced that she will come and eagerly awaits the promised day. Finally the wedding night arrives, but he is still without word from her. Since he has, however, made up his mind to leave this world, he determines to die alone.

The first scene, printed in the Viennese periodical *Der Merker* in May, 1912, on the occasion of Schnitzler's fiftieth birthday, shows Hans alone in his room at twilight. His friend, the poet Franz, comes with a young lady to invite him to an outdoor excursion, but finds him adamant to the lure of spring. In verses resembling those of Hofmannsthal's Claudio in *Der Tor und der Tod*, Hans voices his complete disappointment with life. He is tired of unstable emotions and insincere relations, and is ready to leave this world. His lonely musings are interrupted by Agathe, who appears in her bridal veil. Disgust has overtaken her in the midst of her wedding to the brutal but wealthy merchant, and she, too, is determined to seek in death an escape from the pain of existence. In order to enjoy their last hour to the utmost, they sit down to a feast. They eat and drink, while the fragrance of spring enters through an open window. Suddenly he warns her: "You have been drinking poison!" She cries out in horror. He reassures her: he was merely testing her. Now, the real poison draught is to be quaffed. They clink glasses. He drinks. She lets her glass fall. As he dies, full of scorn for her weakness, she rushes back into life.

The second act, of which only a part was completed, was to depict the wedding, the disappearance of the bride, the excitement of the guests, the wrath of the bridegroom, the return of Agathe without the costly veil, and the resulting scandal. The role of the bridegroom is assigned to a coarse merchant, Demeter Stanzides, who later reappears as a refined gentleman in *Der Weg ins Freie* and in *Das weite Land*.

The third act was to bring the couple to the room of the dead officer, in order to recover the missing veil, and was to end with the death of Agathe at the hands of the bridegroom.

While in the midst of writing the second act, Schnitzler must have become aware of certain weaknesses inherent in his plot, for he failed to continue with his composition. He must have felt that he had not sufficiently motivated certain acts of his characters; as, for example, Agathe's marriage to the merchant in spite of her love for the officer. He possibly wondered whether transposing the action to another century would not give him greater freedom in developing his material. If the drama were to take place during the Renaissance, and if a duke were substituted for Demeter Stanzides, then, the behavior of Agathe would be perfectly intelligible. In spite of her love for Hans, she could not fail to be impressed by a duke's majestic presence. In addition, pressure could be brought to bear upon her by her parents, who would be overwhelmed by the great honor bestowed upon them.

In September, 1898, Schnitzler, therefore, began to recast his material so as to give it a Renaissance coloring. In order that the sudden changes in the relations between his people during the course of a single night might assume added significance, the dramatist cast the shadow of death over all the happenings of the play.

Bologna is encircled by the troops of Cesare Borgia, and even its ruler, Lionardo Bentivoglio, has abandoned all hope of successful resistance. The fall of the town and the doom of its inhabitants are expected on the morrow. The last night has come. No longer need any one fear the consequences of any act. Hence, all seek to enjoy each precious moment in its utmost intensity. In the palace and gardens of Duke Bentivoglio, the Bacchic orgies reach their height. The Duke himself joins in the revelry and intoxication. He is fascinated by a young girl, Beatrice Nardi, whom he has met for the first time a few hours earlier, just as she was about to wed a young artisan, Vittorino Monaldi. Free of all responsibility for the future, he begins to woo her. She is willing to follow him as his wife, but not as his mistress. Without a moment's hesitation, he sends for a priest to perform the marriage ceremony, and invites the entire youth of Bologna as his guests. The feast that begins soon after in such riotous fashion is, however, to end before dawn in silence and awe.

Little does the Duke know the woman whom he has chosen as his mate. Nor does she know herself or her reactions to any given situation before she is compelled to face it. Beatrice Nardi glides from person to person, from experience to experience, without remorse or pride. Love and delight are about her; sorrow and death are in her wake. Yet, she herself is innocent of either good or evil intentions. She is betrothed to an honest and simple-minded artisan, when her beauty inflames the poet Filippo Loschi and causes him to exercise his charm over her. From that moment all other beings are as lifeless marionettes in her eyes, and he becomes the center of her world. An apparently insignificant incident, however, suffices to change the direction of her thoughts and the course of her fate. The Duke happens to glance up at her window, as he is riding down the street; and during that sultry summer afternoon she dreams of herself in his arms. Filippo, her lover, to whom she afterwards innocently relates this dream, is so horrified at her imaginary infidelity that he sends her away from him. He tells her that dreams are lustful desires devoid of courage—insolent wishes that retreat before the light of day into remote corners of the soul, only to emerge again stealthily during the night. He insists that nothing could purify her image in his heart, unless it be a common death.

Reluctantly she leaves her lover; and in the following hours she becomes, in turn, the bride of Vittorino and the cause of his death, the wife of the Duke and the source of his disgrace. She is impelled by irresistible longing to escape from the ducal wedding feast to the house of the poet; and a few minutes later she flees from this very house in horror, after having brought about Filippo's suicide. She experiences more in a single day than others do in a lifetime; and, before the following dawn breaks, she is tired of exciting adventures and ready for the end. The Duke, who is expected to punish her apparent faithlessness, realizes the difficulty of judging and condemning: "Were you not, Beatrice, merely a child who played with a crown because it glistened, with a poet's soul because it was full of riddles, with a youth's heart because it was presented to you? But we are all too severe to tolerate such an act. Each of us wanted to be, not alone your sole plaything—nay more, your entire world; and so we called your actions deception and crime. You, however, were but a child."

The mild attitude of the Duke is typical of the tolerance displayed by Schnitzler's husbands toward the infidelity of their wives. It contrasts sharply with the cruel attitude of philanderers, such as Filippo, who abuse their sweethearts for past errors and even involuntary dreams. The tolerance displayed by the maturer and wiser men results from the realization on their part that love is more than the delightful game in which Anatol, and Fritz Lobheimer, and Julian Fichtner engage. It is a giving rather than a taking; it is a transferring of one's center of interest from the ego to another personality. "To love means to exist for someone else," says Sala, in *Der einsame Weg*. "What has that which one of our kind brings into the world to do with love? Our mixture of jolliness, deceit, tenderness, villainy, and passion may call itself love, but it really isn't love. Did we ever bring a sacrifice from which our sensuality, or our conceit, did not profit? Did we ever hesitate to lie or to betray decent people, if we could thereby gain an hour of joy or lust? Did we ever stake our tranquillity or our lives—no, I don't mean for some frivolous whim or other—in order to further the well-being of some person who gave herself to us?"

Unlike the youthful philanderers, Schnitzler's older men conclude that to love means to be a citadel of refuge for the beloved—a home from which the beloved may, perhaps, sally forth, if the lure of adventure should entice her away, but to which, under all circumstances, she ought to be permitted to return. This attitude, first vaguely touched upon in the narrative *Die Frau des Weisen*, in 1896, is treated from different angles in numerous plays and stories throughout the succeeding decades. As Schnitzler grows older, his characters mature with him. The frivolous bachelor and the unmarried girl cease to occupy the center of his attention. He becomes interested, to an ever increasing extent, in the relations between husband and wife—relations that are seldom stabilized by a mere wedding ceremony. Some of his finest works, to which we are about to turn, deal with the problems and ills of married life.

CHAPTER III

THE ILLS OF MARRIAGE

THE most tragic chord struck by Schnitzler is that of loneliness—a chord that resounds from his earliest narratives, as well as from his last dramas. We human beings, he feels, are almost predestined to live alone and to die alone. During our all too few years on earth, however, we make frantic efforts to escape from our absolute solitude. In work we find a drug that helps us to forget, but it is only during the intoxication of love that we are enabled really to break through the bars that separate individual existences. Schnitzler's men—cool, rational, ironic—may, at best, resign themselves to work and forgetfulness. His women, on the other hand, do, at times, bridge the gulf between soul and soul; and in ecstatic abandon they do attain perfect communion with the All. His women are, on the whole, more courageous than his men. The latter hesitate, deliberate, weigh all possible risks, and seek to postpone their decisions. If forced to act, they try to minimize their responsibility and to avoid every possible consequence of their act. The women, on the contrary, answer the call of life heroically, brave all dangers readily, and lose themselves successfully in others. They, thus more easily, experience true love.

Western civilization for a long time emphasized male superiority, and thereby made man ever more self-centered and egotistic. While woman has retained her capacity to respond naturally, naively, instinctively, man has been handicapped by an overabundance of rationalization. Schnitzler's women want love. Schnitzler's men offer understanding. Schnitzler's women are, therefore, generally dissatisfied with their ideal husbands and seek dangerous experiences outside of the marital relationship. They prefer cruel, unrelenting Anatols and Casanovas to wise professors and physicians. Schnitzler's husbands, and even prospective husbands, understand this behavior, too, and tolerate it. Their insight into the soul's complexity prevents their flaring-up either in strong resentment or in intense passion.

Schnitzler's narrative *Die Frau des Weisen*, published in 1896, is one of his earliest studies of married people. The hero of the story is a professor, at whose house a young student has been residing for some time. On the day that the youth is to leave town permanently, the professor's wife, who hitherto has apparently taken only a maternal interest in the student, enters his room to bid him farewell. Suddenly, overcome by a strong wave of emotion, she bends down to him and bestows upon him a passionate, unmaternal kiss, that fills him with shudders of joy. The next moment, just as she buries her face in his hands and the fragrance of her hair begins to intoxicate him, he notices that the door is opening slightly. The professor peers in, and then silently retreats without having been seen by the woman. In consternation the youth leaves the home. His vivid imagination conjures up all sorts of horrible scenes that must be taking place after his hasty departure. In time, however, he calms down and forgets the incident almost entirely. Seven years later, while at a Danish bathing resort, he again meets the professor's wife. The atmosphere of sultry summer days and moonlight nights once more weaves tender bonds between the two. They are being drawn ever closer to each other. Just then the young man learns that the woman has never found out that she was seen in his arms by her husband. The wise professor has been silent throughout the following years, and has pardoned her without a single word of reproach. The young man feels that it would be outrageous under these circumstances to betray again that kind, understanding person. The professor's forgiveness has rendered his wife immune, and so, for a second time, the former student flees, abashed.

From this tale, one might rashly deduce the conclusion that the author believes the attitude of the wise professor commendable in all such situations. But Schnitzler never generalizes. As if to prove the danger of drawing hasty conclusions from any one specific case, he writes a one-act play in which three characters, all such to those in the narrative, are presented in a similar relation to one another, and in which the husband's silence serves only to encourage the lovers. This play appeared in 1898 under the title *Die Gefährtin*.

Professor Robert Pilgram is married to a woman twenty years younger than himself. From the first he has had no illusions about her. He knows that, because of the difference in their ages, she will probably some day become faithless to him. But he feels that they may, at least, share a few years of bliss together, and that these will compensate for possible future unpleasantnesses. At the worst, he has his work to fall back upon. Hence, it does not shock him to discover before long that his wife is carrying on an affair with his assistant, Dr. Alfred Hausmann. He himself is old, and the two young people really belong to each other. He waits for them to come to him to ask him for their freedom. He cannot understand their hesitating. He himself is too timid to suggest this step to them or even to hint that he knows of their illicit relations. And so the years pass.

When the play opens, the professor's wife has just died, and he is waiting for Alfred to return from an interrupted vacation. He is almost sorry for the young man. He feels that the assistant may break down with grief, and is prepared to comfort him. Alfred arrives. His sorrow is more conventional than sincere. He has just announced his engagement while on his vacation. However, he has been wooing his fiancée for the past two years, even while carrying on his affair with Mrs. Pilgram. When the professor learns these new facts, he turns indignantly upon the young man and asks him to leave the house: "I would have raised you from the ground, if pain had broken you. I would have gone with you to her grave, if it were your beloved who lay buried there. You, however, made her your harlot, and filled this house up to the ceiling with filth and lies. I am so disgusted—that's why, yes, that's why I drive you out of here." But the professor then learns, to his dismay, that his wife knew of the coming engagement, that she looked upon it as something inevitable, and that, in spite of all this, she continued her affair. The lovers never would have asked the husband for their freedom, for they really had all the freedom they wanted.

We thus see that, while the professor in Die Frau des Weisen, who silently forgave his wife and her lover, was wise, the professor in *Die Gefährtin*, who in a similar situation acted in exactly the same way, was a fool. What is right in one specific instance may be wrong in another parallel instance. Generalizing about human conduct is unsafe. Schnitzler avoids it. After he has treated a problem from one angle and offered an apparently successful solution to it, he is tempted to revert to the same problem from another angle and to demonstrate the absurdity of the very same solution. He holds that there are no panaceas for life's ills. Every human being is unique. Every "sickness" in the relations between people must, therefore, be carefully studied and diagnosed, before a specific medicine can be prescribed. The medicine that cures in one case may act as a poison that kills in another. Schnitzler's remedies make no pretense of being universally applicable. They apply only to the individuals under examination.

In the narrative *Ein Abschied*, which appeared in 1895, Schnitzler examines the reactions of a lover who, after waiting in vain for his beloved, a married woman, learns that she cannot keep her appointment because she is mortally ill. He wants to go to her but does not dare, because he fears to compromise her. When he hears of her death, however, he can control himself no longer. He enters her home and mingles, unnoticed, with the mourners. He looks into her pale face and thinks of the hours not so long ago when he held her in his arms. Suddenly he hears a sobbing voice thanking him for his sympathy, and he feels the hand of the husband clasping his. He cannot tell the broken-hearted man the truth. He dares not assert that he, and not the husband, is the person to whom the wife really belonged. With bowed head, he leaves the home; and, as he looks back at the dead woman for the last time, he imagines that he sees a scornful smile on her lips. This smile seems to chide him for his cowardly behavior in disowning her.

A similar illicit relation between a young man and a married woman, in which the surviving member attempts to disown the dead partner, recurs in Schnitzler's beautiful tale *Die Toten Schweigen* (1897). Here again, a lover is waiting impatiently for his beloved. She cannot come until her husband, a physician, has left home for a conference. Finally she appears, trembling with excitement, lest she be recognized. The two hail a cab and drive out to the suburbs. The lover admonishes her for her lateness. She offers excuses. He wants her to give up her double existence with its nervous strain and constant fear. She hesitates. She cannot make up her mind to leave her kind husband and her comfortable home. She quiets her Franz with kisses. Meanwhile, a storm is brewing, and the drunken coachman has difficulty in groping through the dark night. While the lovers are in the midst of an embrace, the coach jolts violently and overturns. The occupants are hurled out upon the pavement. When the woman recovers from her daze, she sees her Franz lying wounded and unconscious beside her. She sends the coachman to telephone for an ambulance. As she bends over the young man, she realizes that he is already dead. She shudders at the thought of her predicament: a woman alone with a corpse. People will soon come and question her. The police will want to find out who she is and what she is doing here. If only she could remain unknown! What a scandal, if anyone should discover that she, a respectable wife and mother, was the mistress of the dead person! The thought of flight occurs to her. Franz is beyond help. Why should she needlessly ruin her life and reputation? A few hundred paces off this road, and she will be safe. No one, then, could possibly associate her with the accident. She flees through the dark night and arrives home just before her husband's return. She sits down to tea with him. He tells her of the medical conference with his colleagues. She pretends to listen, but all the while she is thinking of her miraculous escape. How wonderful it is to be alive in one's cosy home! How fine it is to see one's child! Suddenly, a horrible possibility crosses her mind. What if her lover were not dead! What if he were to recover his senses and to ask for her! But no, he must be dead; he is surely dead; and dead men tell no tales. Unconsciously, she utters her last thought aloud. Her husband repeats her words. Now she knows that her secret is out. In his eyes she reads that she can no longer conceal anything from him whom she has betrayed for years; and a great peace comes over her, as though a load were, at last, to be lifted from her.

Schnitzler's fine artistic sense makes him break off the story at this climax, since our imagination can, without difficulty, supply the conclusion. We know from the other works of the same period, such as *Die Frau des Weisen* and *Die Gefährtin*, that the husband, who is a professor and physician, will probably act just as his colleagues have. He will listen with tolerant understanding to his wife's confession. He will not only forgive her, but he may even use all the logic and eloquence at his command to soothe her troubled conscience.

Only ignorant husbands believe that the possession of a woman through marriage is a guarantee of her love. Only unthinking husbands assume that a wife's avoidance of all forbidden paths is a proof of her fidelity. One such stupid husband is the armorsmith Cyprian, in the one-act play *Paracelsus* (1897). Married for thirteen years to the beautiful Justina, Cyprian boasts of his success in winning and retaining her affections. He jeers at Paracelsus, the Renaissance physician and magician, who, also, was at one time interested in Justina, and who must have been rejected when courting her thirteen years before. For, after the incident

Paracelsus had left town, and from that time until his return to his native Basel, he had led the life of a roaming, unstable charlatan. Stung by the taunts of the complacent husband, Paracelsus hypnotizes Justina and commands her to speak, until sundown, the truth and nothing but the truth. To Cyprian's dismay, the truth turns out differently from what he expected. His wife reveals to him that, on many a night when he held her in his arms, her thoughts were far away from him. She discloses that she has loved Paracelsus for a much longer time than anyone has imagined. She tells the "wonder-working" physician: "Thirteen years ago, when you left without a word of farewell and without any intention of returning, I thought I would have to die. Had you come back the night on which you departed, I would gladly have given you everything for which you might have asked—even though I knew that the morrow would have taken you from me forever—so much did I love you! Who knows how many windows in the town are open every night for those who never come!" Even after these many years of married life, Justina still does not feel sure of herself. A young squire, whose advances she has indignantly rejected, comes to take leave of her. While under the effect of the hypnotic command to speak the absolute truth, she tells him it is a good thing for him that he must go so quickly. "Had you stayed here even one more night, we would have parted less innocent. I still feel the last shudders of youth. Spring flatters, and beauty lures. Therefore, it is good that you go as quickly as possible. For alas, where would it all end? A little joy, and a great deal of fear and remorse. All this I am now spared." Cyprian is overwhelmed by these strange revelations. Chastened in his pride, he wonders which is the real Justina—the simple creature who has walked at his side all these years, or the complex bundle of emotions and impulses that came to the fore when the censoring rational faculties were dulled. He asks Paracelsus to unravel the mystery and the confusion; to state definitely whether the scene just witnessed is to be taken seriously, or whether it is to be regarded merely as a conjurer's play. Paracelsus wisely replies: "It was play. What else should it be? What is not play that we carry on here below, though it may seem great and deep. One person plays with wild soldier hordes; another, with superstitious fools; still another, with suns and stars, I play with human souls. Only he who looks for a meaning finds one. Dream life and wakeful life, truth and fiction flow into each other. Certainty is nowhere to be found. We know nothing of others, nothing of ourselves. We play always. He who realizes this is wise."

Human relations have their "sicknesses" even as human beings do. Sometimes these "sicknesses" may be staved off. At other times they must be allowed to run their course. If recovery follows, everyone concerned should feel relieved, and should not mutter obsolete words, such as "immorality" or "crime."

Would marriage, then, according to Schnitzler, be a healthier and happier institution if the contracting parties, assured of mutual understanding and forgiveness, were to agree to tell each other the truth about temptations that might cross their paths? Not necessarily, the dramatist replies. In two plays, *Die Frau mit dam Dolche* (1900) and *Zwischenspiel* (1904), the husbands and wives on their wedding day promise each other to confess any "extra-marital" longings that might arise. In the former play, confession does not hinder the woman's yielding subsequently to the tempter; while in the latter play, constant self-probing tends to bring on the very malady against which they were guarding themselves.

Pauline, the heroine of *Die Frau mit dem Dolche*, is happily married. She loves and respects her husband. She rejoices in his artistic triumphs and would be miserable, were she to be separated from him for a long time. At the same time, owing to the complexity of human creatures, there are, also, moments when she hates her beloved husband, and when she is capable of betraying him. She experiences just such a moment of weakness when it flashes upon her mind that her whole fate may, perhaps, signify no more to her husband than an interesting theme for a play, while she means so much to young Leonhard that he would gladly sacrifice his life for her. In accordance with her wedding promise not to keep any secrets from her husband, she reveals to her mate the temptation to which she fears she will fall a victim; and both, believers in preventive medicines, determine to avoid the threatening emotional storm by leaving for Italy. Pauline argues logically that for the sake of a so-called hour of bliss, it is hardly worth risking her pleasant, calm existence, or perhaps even jeopardizing her very life. Armed with this sane reasoning, she goes to see Leonhard for the last time, in order to bid him adieu. Her husband knows of this rendezvous; but, like all tolerant "Schnitzler" husbands, he does not feel that he has a right to limit his wife's freedom in any way. At this final meeting, however, the spell of Leonhard's physical personality reasserts itself; and, though Pauline struggles hard to resist his fascination, she does succumb in the end. During the very moment when she tries to hold him off, he asks her: "Why do your glances become moist as I speak to you, and why do your lips long for mine as we stand calmly here near each other?" Pauline, tortured by conflicting emotions, truthfully replies: "What is the purpose of these questions, Leonhard? I deny nothing, for denial would be disgusting and cowardly. But I should be guilty of an even more abominable lie, if I were to tell you that I love you. There was never a moment when I myself believed it; and yet, there was a moment when I was ready to be yours. You missed that moment, and it will not return. Nor will you ever learn when it was. Yes, such is life! It's no disgrace for me, and no credit to you. It has happened millions of times. The only difference is that other women in my place say: 'I cherish for you the love of a sister—of a friend. Ask no other.' I, however, say to you, Leonhard, that I feel toward you anything else you might possibly wish me to feel, but not friendship—by God, no!" Pauline senses herself in the grip of mighty forces whose bidding it is useless to try to resist. She is made to realize that neither her husband, nor her lover, nor she herself has much voice in determining the ebb and flow of their emotional lives. A "super-individual" power impels them; an arm of fate, that cannot be cajoled or flattered, drives them on.

In a dream scene that flashes through her mind, Pauline is transported to an earlier century. She sees herself experiencing, in a previous incarnation, the epilogue of an adventure similar to the one into which she is about to be drawn. As Paolo, the wife of the Renaissance painter Remigio, she has spent the night with Lionardo, while her husband is away at the court of Cosimo di Medici. When morning comes, Lionardo insists upon remaining at her home and laying claim to her. Paolo, however, spurns him, for she still regards herself as the faithful wife of Remigio. To her it seems a matter of minor importance with whom one sleeps, but it is a matter of utmost importance with whom one spends the waking hours. A woman's yielding to an hour of lust, or the common satisfaction of physical desires, confers no rights upon the man; nor does such an experience harbor any promise for the future. When her husband, Remigio, arrives, Paolo calmly tells him of her night's adventure, as though she were mentioning some trivial occurrence. He, in turn, receives her confession with equal unconcern. He simply asks Lionardo to leave. When the lover, incensed at being treated as a mere, accidental tool, still insists on intruding upon the waking hours of the happily married couple, and even goes so far as to threaten Remigio's life and reputation, Paolo rushes to her husband's defense and stabs Lionardo.

This scene of centuries ago passes like lightning through the mind of Pauline, as Leonhard reminds her that she will not leave for Italy until the following morning, and that he will be expecting her in the evening. Pauline hesitates a moment longer. Then, aware of the possible tragic consequences of her decision, but also aware of the hopelessness of struggling against the call of the blood, she murmurs assent. The absolute honesty supposedly prevailing in her relations to her husband do not suffice to save her from the physical allurements of a seducer.

Is there, then, no assurance against emotional instability? Are there no unassailable barriers that can be placed in the way of temptation? Must all efforts at effecting successful resistance be abandoned? Schnitzler's mature heroes and heroines grope for a satisfactory substitute for the old-fashioned type of marriage. Their groping leads them into many strange experiments. Their quest for a morality better adapted to the psychology of twentieth century beings, opens up fields well worth exploring.

CHAPTER IV

THE QUEST FOR NEW MORALS

THROUGH the mouths of dramatic heroes, Schnitzler repeatedly expresses his doubt that it is possible to have absolute truthfulness between man and woman in all of life's circumstances. Yet, even if it were possible, he remains skeptical as to its desirability. A marriage, in which husband and wife would confide to each other every illicit thought and every unfaithful stirring of the heart, would not be a happy union of permanent duration. The very effort to guard against such thoughts or emotions would hasten their appearance. The very desire to communicate them would magnify their importance and aggravate their ill effects.

As an object lesson Schnitzler presents, in *Zwischenspiel* (1904), an ultra-modern couple who undertake to build a home on the pillars of truth and freedom, and who finally must confess that no lasting structure can be erected on such unstable pillars.

For the musical conductor Amadeus and the opera star Cäcilie, the marriage ceremony to which they submit is, perhaps, mainly a concession to public opinion. In their own eyes, their union is cemented more strongly by common interests and mutual affection. They are comrades, coworkers, and lovers. As rational beings, they can conceive a time when they might cease to share their love life, when, indeed, they might be more attracted to some other person or persons. In such an event, they would still remain friends. They would still pursue the same profession. She would continue to be the inspiration of his musical compositions, and he would remain her favorite operatic conductor. At all times they would be honest with each other, and they would never fail to consult each other about their emotional problems. For seven years they live according to these principles. Loving each other, they are never conscious of outside lures. A child is born to them, and both delight in caring for it. When Amadeus boasts that his ideal marriage has been so successful because it is based on the sound principle of absolute frankness, the poet Albertus Rhön hints that probably nothing has transpired which was worth concealing; and he prophetically predicts the breakdown of this elaborate system of assurance against fate. Amadeus remarks that he and his wife have never challenged fate with a sense of too great security. Albertus wisely replies that fate may feel itself challenged by doubt, as well as by overbearing confidence. "At any rate," counters Amadeus, "there is a certain satisfaction in knowing that, come what may, one will not be caught unawares." Albertus, however, believes that a greater satisfaction may be attained, if a person makes up his mind not to be caught at all—in other words, if he throws overboard his theories of freedom and wards off all influences that might jeopardize his marital happiness or that might subject his mate to temptation. Amadeus cannot agree with this view: "Do you think that much is won by such defense-mechanism? Would you not rather hold that to fight temptations while the soul longs for them, is the worst of all lies and the most dangerous; and that one may more easily emerge unscathed from perilous adventures than from unfulfilled desires?" Albertus remains unconvinced, and his skepticism finds justification in coming events.

The eagerness of Amadeus to dwell constantly upon marriage problems indicates that he is not altogether happy in his marital state. After seven years, there has come about a considerable apathy in the sense life of the couple. As a result, their immunity to outside lures has begun to wear off. Cäcilie notices that he is not indifferent to the looks of a female pupil, Countess Friedericke; and he suspects that she does not wholly disdain the attentions of their friend, Prince Sigismund. The hour which husband and wife expect and fear seems to have arrived. Unwilling to restrict each other's freedom, both pretend to adjust themselves calmly to the new situation. Instead of preventing Cäcilie from gliding into unknown adventures, as she half hoped he would, Amadeus urges her to follow the dictates of the heart, even as he himself plans to do. When Cäcilie interprets his attitude as signifying that all is over between them, he protests vigorously. He does not understand why they cannot continue to practice their profession together, since she will always be the best source for his inspiration, and he will still remain her best accompanist. Nor does he see the need of rendering their child fatherless. Surely they ought to continue to rear their child in common. For its sake, and as a matter of convenience, might it not even be best to go on living in the same quarters? Cäcilie points out that such an arrangement would probably prove impossible, since hereafter they will have secrets to keep from each other. Amadeus disputes her logic. Why can they not confide in each other as before? Surely they will remain the best of comrades. Outwardly there need be hardly any change in their relations. Inwardly, however, a certain embarrassment and nervousness will have disappeared. Amadeus embraces Cäcilie for the last time as his beloved, and then he shakes her hand as his welcome new friend. The two comrades separate to leave on their vacations. Amadeus makes immediate use of his improved opportunities by entering into an affair with the countess; and then, tiring of her, he drowns his dissatisfaction with himself in affairs with other women. Meanwhile, Cäcilie vainly hopes for a visit from him, and writes long letters day after day to him. When her vacation is over, she celebrates artistic triumphs as a guest-singer in Berlin. In the fall she returns to Vienna. Amadeus finds her completely changed. Her voice is fuller and richer. Her eyes burn with passion and promise. She confesses to her comrade and nominal husband that all wishes which formerly glided off her as from an iron coat-of-mail, so long as she was conscious of marital responsibilities, now penetrate her body and soul more easily, and make her tremble and glow. The earth now seems to her full of enticing adventures; heaven seems to radiate flames; and she envisages herself standing with outstretched arms, waiting for something to happen. She can imagine herself in her present mood succumbing to an unscrupulous seducer. At her words, Amadeus catches fire. He wants to be that seducer. He finds her more beautiful than ever before. He divines that she can bestow greater bliss than he has known in many a year. In spite of his fine resolution to be merely her friend and comrade, in spite of having given up his claims as husband, and in spite of her warning not to enter upon such a perilous experience, he rouses her blood, intoxicates her senses, and seduces her.

On the following morning, Amadeus is torn with jealousy. He will not tolerate a possible rival. Asserting his rights as husband, he challenges to a duel Prince Sigismund, whom he suspects of being his wife's lover. He is overwhelmed with joy when he learns that his suspicions are groundless. Cäcilie calls his attention to the contradiction in his views. On the one hand, he expects her to treat his own escapades as trivialities; on the other hand, he himself is ready to kill or be killed because of a mere suspicion of infidelity on her part.

Both realize that pure friendship between man and woman is a most dangerous experiment, for, where souls understand each other too well, they have a tendency to draw the senses along in their wake. They also realize that eternal fidelity is, perhaps, no less a myth. Human beings can offer no guarantee as to the flow of their emotions. No person can be sure of himself, and certainly he cannot be sure of others. Instability is inherent in human nature. Truth is an illusory ideal that married people can never live up to. "Though everything else may have been true," says Cäcilie, "the fact that we both took the matter so lightly, when you confessed your passion for the countess and I, my attraction for Sigismund—that was not the truth. Had we hurled into each other's face our anger, our chagrin, our despair, instead of acting the role of calm and considerate beings, then we would have been truthful—but we were not."

Freedom from responsibility is, thus, no insurance against marital difficulties, but on the contrary it opens the door wide to every lure. The intermezzo in the relations of the ultra-modern couple will probably repeat itself again and again, so long as the man and the woman are not conscious of mutual duties and responsibilities. The doctrine of *laissez faire* in family life must lead to tragic consequences. Cäcilie's liberation from duty exposed her to temptation. The call of her child brought her back to her senses. Sufficient work for the man, or the care of a home and a child for a woman, will avert many a domestic tragedy. The mature dramatist, after meandering along fascinating, amoral bypaths, does not shun this return to an old conservative doctrine. In a symbolic tale, published in 1911 under the title *Die Hirtenflöte* but conceived years earlier, Schnitzler, again, violently rebukes a tolerant husband who failed to keep his wife from falling into temptation. The stargazer Erasmus thinks he has attained the height of wisdom when he suggests to his young wife, Dionysia, that she ought not to avoid answering the call of adventure whenever it resounds in her ears. After deep meditation it occurs to this sage that neither he nor she has a right to assume that her tenderness is real love; her unerring devotion, real faith; and her equanimity of soul, real happiness. She has never been tested in the storm and stress of an eventful life. Her many possibilities are still dormant within her. The fact that her conduct is above reproach augurs little as to the state of her inner self, since this conduct may have been dictated by her fear of the consequences that might befall her should she ever break her marriage vows. If, however, he were to liberate her from this fear; if he were to renounce all his rights over her—the right to warn her, the right to hold her back, the right to punish her; if he were to permit her to follow every whim and every longing, no matter where they might lead her; if he were, finally, to assure her that she would always find her home and bed and board unchanged whenever she might return, and that no word of reproach or query would taunt her, then, and then only, would he be certain that her behavior was the expression of her deepest being—then only could he rejoice whole-heartedly in their love.

In the midst of these meditations, the tones of a shepherd's flute come up from the valley. Erasmus notices that Dionysia's face is lighting up with curiosity and eagerness. He thereupon directs her to follow this first lure and all succeeding ones until her destiny has been fulfilled and she has undergone all the experiences through which she was fated to go.

Unrestrained by responsibilities of any kind, Dionysia becomes, in turn, the mistress of the shepherd, the companion of an industrialist, the prey of a rebel horde, the beloved of a count, and the paramour of a prince. She knows the joy of motherhood, and the grief that follows a child's death. After many days she finds herself in the vicinity of her long deserted home. She sees the door still open, as though she were still expected to return. Erasmus is imperturbably busy stargazing. Without a word of rebuke, he bids her welcome. At her astonished question if he does not shudder to receive her after all she has lived through, he calmly replies: "You have lived your life, Dionysia. You stand before me purer than all the others who breathe in the murky mist of their wishes. You know who you are. Why should I shudder at seeing you?"

"I know who I am?" she exclaims. "I know as little about myself as when you made me leave you. In the limited world, which you, at first, prepared for me and in which everything was regulated by duty, it was not granted to me to find myself. In the boundless world into which you sent me and in which everything lured me on, I had to lose myself. No, I do not know who I am."

"What is the matter, Dionysia?" asks Erasmus. "Do you want to upbraid me for doing what no sage among lovers has ever dared to do—what no lover among sages ever brought himself to the point of doing?"

"You, a sage?" she counters angrily. "You who did not realize that to every human creature only a very narrow strip has been allotted to understand and to fulfill his being? There it is that the unique mystery of his personality—that mystery which is born but once in him and which never returns—flows in unison with the supreme laws of the divine and human order. You, a lover? You who did not, on that distant morn, descend into the valley to break a flute, the tones of which threatened your beloved with seduction? Your heart was tired, Erasmus. That is why you let me depart without beginning the struggle which was then not yet lost. And your spirit was caught in the rigid strangle hold of words. That is why you thought you could capture in the depthless mirror of a formula the immense fullness of life and the interplay of millions of forces."

When Erasmus tries to appease her and to assure her that she will find undisturbed calm and benevolent understanding in her former home, she turns from him in scorn: "Had you been horrified by the breath of the thousand fates that float about my forehead, I could have remained, and our souls would, perhaps, have been hammered together in the glow of ineffable pain. As it is, however, I shudder more at the grotesque visage of your wisdom than at all the masks and marvels of this world."

Erasmus, the seer, loses his wife by refusing to ward off temptations from her. The passive philosopher is unsuccessful in his marital experiment. And yet, he had but followed consistently the ideal once prescribed by his creator, Schnitzler: that to love means to be a citadel of refuge for the beloved—a citadel from which the beloved may sally forth when the lure of adventure beckons to her, and to which she may return at any time. Apparently the dramatist was beginning to doubt the adequacy of this definition of love. This doubt finds its best expression in the one-act play *Das Bacchusfest*, published in 1915 but begun in December, 1911, soon after the appearance of *Die Hirtenflöte*. In this comedy, Schnitzler depicts a husband who, unlike Erasmus, struggles with the tempter and thereby regains, at the very last moment, his wife's affection and admiration.

The scene of the encounter is laid in the waiting-room of a railroad station. Felix Staufner has telegraphed his wife, Agnes, that he is returning from his vacation. He has received a reply from her that she will meet him en route. It is not her intention, however, to go back with him to Vienna. For, while he has been away for six weeks at the seashore, apparently wrapped up in his literary work and therefore neglecting her, she has felt herself being drawn towards Dr. Guido Wernig. This young man has now come with her, and together they await the arrival of Felix's train. They plan to ask the husband to free Agnes, because she does not want to lead a life of lies and guilt. The lovers are certain that Felix, in his noble and magnanimous way, will raise no objections. When the husband enters the waiting-room, he takes in the entire situation at a glance. Yet, he pretends to be overjoyed at the meeting. He thanks the young man for accompanying Agnes to the station. Without giving either of them an opportunity to broach their all-important topic, Felix continues to talk of his work and his problems. He confesses that he is not quite finished with his manuscript, because he needs his wife's advice. He hints that he is tired of loneliness, and that he would like to travel with her and to devote the following few weeks to her. With each ensuing moment, his personality begins to recast its old spell upon Agnes. Finally he wins her over completely. He is then in a position to suggest to Guido that he take care not to miss the next train. Abashed, Guido leaves them, and the reunited couple remain in Salzburg. Neither husband nor wife will ever forget the incident. Moreover, as a result of this experience they have acquired a certain insight. If a storm should ever again assail their calm relations, they will be able to weather it more easily. Their former faith, however, in the absolute stability of their love is irretrievably gone.

We thus see that Schnitzler, who sets out in quest of new morals, ends with a realization of the inadequacy of all moral systems, old and new. No bulwarks can be erected that will guarantee emotional stability under all circumstances. The soul is a vast domain that can never be wholly charted. Innumerable psychic streams course through everyone of us. Sometimes these seethe and rise, overflow and wreak havoc. Often there is very little that we can do to prevent a catastrophe. But, at least, we ought not to shun the effort. Let us act like Felix Staufner, and not like Erasmus, the stargazer.

CHAPTER V

SARDONIC TRUTHS

SCHNITZLER'S answers to various problems affecting the relations between human beings, are presented by him merely as possibilities, and not as final solutions. No sooner is one possibility expressed than he becomes cognizant of another that is equally as plausible. He, then, often succumbs to the temptation of satirizing good-naturedly the very opinion that his hero or heroine has just as fervently defended. Thus, after completing *Der Schleier der Beatrice*, he turns the fire of his wit upon its leading characters, and recasts this tragedy into a play of marionettes. It appears as such in 1910, with an interesting musical setting by the Hungarian composer Ernst von Dohnanyi. Similarly, after a decade of intense preoccupation with the problems of love and marriage, he burlesques his own themes and types in the dramatic sketch *Zum grossen Wurstl*.

Though published in 1904 as a puppet play, it was conceived five years earlier as a one-act tragedy. Schnitzler's manuscripts of 1899 include the following notation: "The husband suspects someone of being his wife's lover and challenges him to a duel. But it is the wrong person. Now the wife comes to the latter with: 'Take me before you fight.' At first the two want to flee. He remains, however, and is shot in the duel."

We see in this outline merely a new combination of favorite Schnitzler themes. Thus, in *Liebelei*, we have a grim husband who challenges to a duel, and kills, his wife's lover at a time when the latter is already engaged in an affair with another woman. In *Zwischenspiel*, we have a similar episode. While Countess Friedericke is carrying on illicit relations with Amadeus, her husband discovers that she was unfaithful to him six months earlier. Thereupon he challenges to a duel the person with whom she has long since broken off her affair.

The act of the woman who throws herself into the arms of the man over whom the shadow of death hangs, also occurs in several of Schnitzler's plays. Thus, Johanna, in *Der einsame Weg*, wants to give herself to the dying Sala. Marie Moser, in *Der Ruf des Lebens*, comes to sweeten the last hours of the doomed lieutenant. When the shadow of death hovers over Bologna, the heroine of *Der Schleier der Beatrice* hastens from her wedding feast to share, before the end, an hour of illicit bliss with the poet Filippo Loschi.

In developing his original concept, Schnitzler soon discovered that the situation, as he envisaged it, was hardly tragic, even though it might involve the hero's death. The unusual position of the young man who finds himself challenged for a pleasant crime of which he is absolutely ignorant, and the peculiar act of the woman who insists upon making him guilty by offering herself to him rather belatedly, could more easily arouse tears of laughter in an audience than tears of sympathy. The characters are, indeed, ideally suited to hilarious comedy. Not only are the characters ridiculous—a husband who challenges the wrong person, a wife who wants to be guilty under all circumstances, and a young man who has to die for someone he hardly knows—but, in addition, other figures capable of heightening the humorous effect easily suggest themselves. The husband's suspicions of his wife's infidelity are likely to be well-founded, and his error will, therefore, be one merely of mistaken identity. Such an error has probably been caused by the fact that the young hero was the friend and companion of the real lover, or lovers. Schnitzler could, thus, introduce two additional characters: the young man's seconds, each of whom would qualify more properly as the butt of the husband's jealousy, and each of whom, conscious of his own guilt, would hardly accept at full value the hero's protestation of innocence. These seconds might get to the point of issuing challenges to the hero in their own behalf, or even of challenging each other.

Furthermore, if Schnitzler set out to depict the doomed young man as wholly innocent, harmless, and respectable, then he ought to have depicted the avenging husband as suspicious, dangerous, brutal, and licentious. To add to the sardonic humor of the situation, the husband might, also, be shown carrying on an affair with the hero's fiancée, so that, logically, the roles of the challenger and the challenged person would be reversed. Such a reversal could be brought about in the course of the play if the husband, discovering his mistake, were to absolve the young hero of all guilt, and if the hero, listening to the proffered explanation, were at the same time to become aware of his adversary's affair with his fiancée.

This turning of the tables is accomplished in the one-act comedy which Schnitzler completed in December, 1899, and which is still unpublished. Eduard has just signed his last will, bequeathing his earthly possessions to his sweetheart, Lucie, when his friends, Albert and Brandis, arrive. He tells them of his coming duel with the perfect marksman Herr von Krögel, and asks them to act as his seconds. Upon learning that Frau von Krögel is the cause of the duel, they, in turn, demand satisfaction and thereby reveal their relations to her. When they go off, the demonic woman appears to confront the astonished hero. She tells him of her lifelong ambition to give herself to a person who has been doomed to certain death. Only such an individual can love without lies or illusions, and without thought of possible consequences. The hero, taken aback by her effrontery, reminds her that he is engaged to a girl whom he intends to marry before he is shot. She urges him not to die innocently, but to take advantage of this final opportunity to become guilty. Just then her husband's voice is heard. She hides in the adjoining room. Herr von Krögel has come to apologize for his error. He tells of his supping at a restaurant with a little girl who twitted him with the remark that his wife was probably, also, betraying him at the same time. He, thereupon, hired a detective to follow his wife's actions. On the third day, when informed that Eduard was her lover, he challenged the young man. Only a few minutes ago did he learn that there was a mix-up, caused by the detective's assumption that the little girl with whom Krögel supped was Frau von Krögel. This explanation convinces Eduard that the girl involved is none other than his dear Lucie; and, in his rage, he determines to repay her in her own coin. When Krögel leaves to keep an appointment with Lucie, Eduard is ready to accept Frau von Krögel's offer. But now she withdraws it, since the young man is no longer under the shadow of death and, therefore, devoid of attraction in her eyes.

This comedy was not published until five years after it was written. Meanwhile it underwent radical changes. The figures were distorted into marionettes. Their speeches parodied wise Schnitzler sayings in other plays. In addition to an increased number of puppets on the stage, many members of the audience participated actively in the performance. The theater director introduced the plot. The poet, distressed at seeing his vision misinterpreted, voiced his disapproval of the actors and the audience. The benevolent theater-goer and the carping critic commented on every phase of the action. Citizens and their families joined in the discussion. Heroes from other plays entered the hall, and added to the confusion. Beer-Hofmann's Graf von Charolais pronounced his fatalistic doctrine that things merely happen, that some inscrutable force impelled him into the theater and was now impelling him to leave. Hermann Bahr's Meister philosophized amidst the deafening uproar. At the height of the confusion an unknown figure appeared with drawn sword. As he waved his blade over the stage, all lights were darkened, and everyone on the stage except himself collapsed. Then, turning to the audience, he asked them to consider what might happen to even the most insolent among them if he were to brandish his sword over their heads.

The final, mystic words of the unknown figure enable us to identify him as Fate. The marionettes believed they were leading a free existence; yet, they were merely pawns in the hands of the poet who pulled their strings. The poet assumed that he alone was free, while the acts of all others were decreed for them; and yet, when the sword of the Unknown flashed above his head, he, too, sank from his eminence. His last words were a plea to the Unknown to reveal himself, but the Unknown remained a nameless mystery even to himself: "I shudder at my might. Is it truth I bring, or night? Do I obey the call of heaven or hell? Is it law or chance that shaped me? Am I a god? . . . a fool?

. . . or a creature fashioned in your image? Am I, I myself—
or only a symbol?" These vague utterances of the Unknown
illustrate, on the one hand, Schnitzler's belief in the omnipo-
tence of fate and, on the other hand, his groping for an
answer to the question: what is fate?
  Because of the omnipresence of this inscrutable factor
of fate, the best mortal plans may go awry. Fate is the
supreme puppet player. A human being, who attempts to
usurp this role, may find his puppets unexpectedly taking
the bit in their own teeth and turning against him. In a one-
act study, entitled *Der Puppenspieler* (1902), Schnitzler
illustrates such a possibility.
  Georg Merklin and Eduard Jagisch, when in their
twenties, were close friends. The former, an aesthetic
epicurean resembling Anatol, felt considerable sympathy
for the latter, who was timid and retiring, especially in the
presence of girls. Georg, therefore, determined upon a peculiar course of action in order to help his friend overcome
his shyness. While carrying on a flirtation with Irene, Georg
induced her companion, Anna, to pretend love for Eduard.
His theory was that, by showering tender affections upon
the naive young man, she would arouse in him greater self-
confidence and courage, which would put him more at ease
in the society of women.
  Eleven years later Georg, the aging aesthete, again
meets Eduard, after the latter's return from America.
Eduard has followed a responsible calling, and has remained
a respectable member of the community. He is happily
married and the father of an eight-year-old boy. Georg
recalls the eventful evening when they met for the last time,
and hints that the shy young man and the blond girl with
the childlike face were then mere puppets in his hands. But

the puppet player soon learns to his dismay that the artificially stimulated flirtation had an unexpected sequel: his two puppets married. From the lips of Anna he hears that he himself was the original object of her love, and that only because of this love did she agree to aid him in his practical joke. She figured on arousing his jealousy, if she whispered sweet words in another man's ear. But Georg paid no attention to her, since he had eyes only for Irene. Anna, thereupon, felt heartily ashamed of her role, and confessed the truth to Eduard. Her desire to make amends developed gradually into love, and they married. Now they are unreservedly happy. Georg is able to contrast their Philistine existence with his own way of living. He insists that irresponsibility and freedom are precious gifts that no person should abandon; and yet, there is a wistful look in his eyes as he kisses the little son of his so-called puppets. Mastering his emotions, he goes out into the cold unknown, while husband and wife sit down to a warm meal in their cosy home and smilingly discuss the aging epicurean, who foolishly believes himself free and master of his fate.

In Georg Merklin we may recognize the successor of the frivolous "Anatol" type, and the forerunner of the lonely "Julian Fichtner" type. As Schnitzler himself enters his forties, his favorite heroes, also, take leave of youth and prepare for the coming of age. They still retain their poise and bravado in the presence of their Philistine friends; they still dream of artistic triumphs in store at some future date; yet, at heart they feel a secret envy of their less gifted, but happier, companions, and they feel a growing skepticism as to their own possible accomplishments. When Georg is reminded of his once promising youth and his barren present, he flares up and defends himself with rhetorical pathos: "Who has told you that I have not become somebody great? Is it necessary that others should notice it? If you were to sell your oboe today, or if your fingers and lips were paralyzed so that you could no longer play the instrument, would you be any less a virtuoso than before? Or, assuming that you didn't like your oboe any more and threw it out of the window because its sound wasn't good enough for you, would you, on that account, cease to be an artist? Would you not rather be more of an artist, if you threw the instrument out of the window because its sound was so dull in comparison with the divine music in your brain? . . . Well, I threw my oboe out. Blockheads exclaimed: 'He gets no ideas!' I let them shout. The real artist can get no ideas, because he has them all within himself—he has inner abundance." These words of Georg, in spite of their fine sound, are less convincing than they were a dozen years earlier, when they were colored by the charm of youth. Whatever inner abundance he may have had, must have been sapped by his overbearing egotism. Any life that is irresponsible beyond a certain age leads to inner impoverishment.

In *Komtesse Mizzi*, a one-act comedy published in 1907, Schnitzler paints with a light, sardonic touch aging aristocrats who refused to shoulder responsibilities and whose entire existence, therefore, shrank to a mere grasping of momentary physical pleasures. There is Count Pazmandy, who has passed his sixtieth birthday but who still is carrying on an affair with a ballet girl. There is his friend, Prince Ravenstein, who can include among his feminine conquests the count's only daughter, Mizzi. Eighteen years earlier, he had seduced the young girl, but he was too cowardly to flee with her, or to make public acknowledgement of his responsibility, when she became a mother. There is Countess Mizzi, who, throughout all the succeeding years, has refused to see her son, because her pride has been wounded by the child's father. While pretending to lead a retired existence, she, too, has found satisfaction in various erotic excursions. These characters continue for decades to associate in the same society; and yet, they really know very little of one another, since each one is encased on all sides by self.

In the same year as the publication of *Komtesse Mizzi*, Schnitzler published the sardonic tale *Der Tod des Junggesellen*. Here, again, people who associate with one another as friends are shown to be largely ignorant of one another's real thoughts and acts. The hero of the story, an aging bachelor, feels death approaching. Thereupon, he sends his servant to call to his bedside his three best friends. They are a physician, a business man, and a poet. When they arrive, he has already breathed his last. A letter is handed to them. It contains his final words of farewell. Eagerly they scan its contents. He informs them that, in spite of his esteem and affection for them, he has, nevertheless, possessed the wives of all three as his mistresses. The reaction of these friends to this startling communication is admirably delineated. The merchant, whose wife is already dead, leaves the room in rage and disgust. The physician, who has left the side of his sleeping wife in order to answer the unexpected summons, remains calm and unmoved. He recalls certain difficult months when he, experiencing the first disappointments in his career, drowned his troubles in questionable adventures. He cannot upbraid his wife, if at that time she, also, took considerable liberties. As the wise healer of broken bodies, as the tolerant consoler of sick souls, he will try to forget the whole incident, and will never mention it to his unsuspecting mate. The poet folds the letter and puts it in his pocket. He, too, will keep silent. But he will make sure that, after his death, his wife shall discover the letter among his literary remains. She will then realize what a noble comrade her husband was; and, grateful to him for his quiet magnanimity, she will whisper sweet words to him when she visits his grave.

The sardonic undertone of this tale recurs in other short stories of the same decade. In *Andreas Thameyers letzter Brief* (1900), the husband of a woman who gave birth to a colored child collects, from various obscure sources, evidence to prove his contention that, in spite of glaring physical differences, he, and he alone, is the child's father. Though he is ready to go to his death in order to demonstrate his unflinching faith in his wife's purity, nevertheless, his very evidence and his very suicide lead the reader to an exactly opposite conclusion. In *Das Schicksal des Freiherrn von Leisenbohg* (1903), tragi-comic scenes from the love life of stage heroes, heroines, and their admirers flit before us. In *Exzentric* (1905), the hero, aware of woman's fickleness, tries to avoid finding out about his sweetheart's infidelities. Yet, all his efforts are unavailing. Though he never encounters her unexpectedly, though he never reads the letters that he accidentally finds on her desk, though he always avoids listening when her name is mentioned, he, nevertheless, cannot escape knowledge of her unfaithfulness. In *Die Fremde* (1903), the hero, who idealizes a young maiden, marries her without knowing much about her inner self. After fourteen days she leaves him; and he, in despair, shoots himself. Soon thereafter she returns, having meanwhile given herself to someone else who did not idealize her but who attracted her fancy.

The sardonic tone also predominates in the comedy *Literatur*, published in 1901. Here Schnitzler satirizes the pseudo-artists who are most at home in the literary cafés of Munich or Vienna. Gilbert and Marguerite have had a commonplace love affair. Instead of forgetting about it after it is over, they each seek to immortalize it in literary form. When Marguerite's fiancée, Baron Clemens, reads her verses about her hanging intoxicated on the neck of someone else, he is thoroughly disgusted. He begs her to give up her writing, now that she is to marry a respectable individual. She promises to do so, but at the same time confesses that her first novel is about to appear in print. Clemens leaves in anger. Just then Gilbert enters. He is on his way to Italy, and has stopped off to bring Marguerite a copy of his novel. She tells him that she, too, is the author of a masterpiece of fiction. This masterpiece includes, as its main theme, a thinly disguised narrative of their love affair. She has been able even to include their correspondence, since in addition to his letters she preserved copies of her own fervent epistles. Gilbert is horrified. His own novel treats of the same episode; he, too, has included in it their entire correspondence. In spite of the fictitious names, every reader would, thus, be able to reconstruct the details of their love life. At this embarrassing moment Clemens returns. He has been to Marguerite's publisher and has had the copies of her novel destroyed, just as they were about to leave the press. He has saved but a single copy, which he intends to keep for his own reading. Since Gilbert's novel may, also, be read by Clemens, Marguerite is in mortal terror of being found out. Acting on a momentary impulse, she snatches the only surviving copy of her novel from the hands of Clemens, and hurls it into the fire. Her fiancée, overwhelmed by her sacrifice, folds her in his arms, while she murmurs words of endearment. Gilbert seizes this moment to make a hasty retreat, and is chagrined that this scene of domestic felicity never occurred to him as a conclusion to his novel.

The best manifestation of Schnitzler's sardonic tone is to be discerned in his *Reigen*, the drama written in the winter of 1896-1897 and, only after long hesitation, printed in 1900 for private circulation among his friends. Not until 1903 did the author consent to its public circulation; and not until 1920 did he approve of its performance on the stage, so greatly did he fear its being misunderstood, or purposely misinterpreted.

Reigen is a series of ten dialogues depicting the roundelay of sexuality. Like the dance of death, which the medieval artists were fond of portraying, the dance of sex may also lay claim to universality. In dispassionate, melancholy conversations, Schnitzler seeks to sketch the pettiness, the brutality, and the absurdity of the sex experience whenever it is purely a physical expression devoid of spiritual meaning. With painful accuracy, he dissects what some people dare to call love but what to him is a ghastly desecration of this sacred term. He points out how much of human life is wasted in pursuit of a moment's pleasure, how little this fleeting experience really should mean to reasoning creatures, and how horrible and inevitable are the disappointments that such moments bring in their wake. With astounding courage, he tears off the mask of hypocrisy that covers sexuality. With amazing frankness, he reveals the technique of the game of sex as played by the many who seek the gratification of physical desires without the participation of their psychic personalities. He shows how the man pursues the woman until he succeeds in arousing in her a dangerous emotional wave, and how he then ruthlessly hurls her away. He portrays the woman for whom, whether she be huntress or hunted, the sensual experience always ends in utter disillusionment. He presents the young person who thinks he is entering on a grand adventure, but who, in the end, feels ridiculous and ashamed. He selects his characters from all social strata and all walks of life, and depicts every one of them as equally pitiable. The dialogues take place between the harlot and the soldier, the soldier and the maid, the maid and the young gentleman, the young gentleman and the young lady, the young lady and her husband, the husband and the sweet maiden, the sweet maiden and the poet, the poet and the actress, the actress and the count, and, finally, the count and the harlot. Schnitzler's humor in these dialogues is bathed in sadness. His mirth is tinged with melancholy. The kind-hearted physician and dramatist sighs over our sick and sorrowful society in which healthy instincts are reduced to selfish lusts, and tragic passions degenerate into petty vices. Though banned by American courts as an immoral book, *Reigen* contains much of the wisdom of the unconventional Viennese thinker.

CHAPTER VI

THE LONELY WAY

FOR almost half a century Arthur Schnitzler wrestled with essential problems, seeking to strip them of their conventional thought associations, to bare them in their universal import, and to extract from them their inner meaning. A study of the sources of Schnitzler's masterpieces and a careful analysis of the stages of composition from the primitive idea until the final, perfected version ought not only to aid in the interpretation of the text, but also to shed considerable light upon the thought processes and the working methods of the author. As a serious artist, Schnitzler rarely permitted a work to be published unless he had assured himself that it rang true to his innermost convictions, and that it had attained the most perfect form which he could give it. At times it could, therefore, happen, as in *Das Märchen*, that a play in its final shape contained a refutation of the thesis which the author originally set out to prove. A five-act tragedy might see the light of day in the form of a novel, as in *Der Weg ins Freie*. On the other hand, a short story might end as an oversized drama or a full-length novel, as *Das weite Land* or *Theresa*. An inadequate solution to a problem might even after the lapse of a quarter of a century still occupy the author's mind, and compel him to attempt a more satisfactory formulation. This applies, for example, to *Der Ruf des Lebens*, a drama which Schnitzler was still busy revising when death came to him.

Schnitzler's first concepts are generally extremely

simple. He usually begins by outlining a single problem to which he seeks a lucid answer. In the course of stating the problem, however, he realizes that there is no single answer that is applicable to all individuals; and that, moreover, no matter how simple the problem may at first appear, it is, finally, somehow interlocked with almost everything else that affects human conduct. To seek its explanation or solution means, therefore, to delve into final causes and ultimate ends, to question God and fate, and to end with a confession of ignorance and impotence. Since this confession is, however, the result of insight into life's complexities, it ought to be preferred to all ready answers and hasty conclusions. Hence, though Schnitzler fails to solve the important questions which he poses, he does remove a maze of prejudices with which these questions are normally surrounded, so that they stare at us in their sphinx-like majesty.

Schnitzler's method of composition is excellently illustrated by *Der einsame Weg*, a drama that underwent unusually radical transformations before its publication in 1903.

The beginning of this play goes back to 1900. In that year Schnitzler jotted down as a possible theme for a drama: "Bachelors. To portray a bachelor, who always let himself be loved, never gave of himself, and merely used up people. Now, his great loneliness to the point of despair. He wants to marry, though knowing that she might become faithless to him. But, at least, he will then have someone. His friend: 'I do not really know why I have always liked you.'"

According to this original concept, the plot would center about an aging egoist, who may be regarded as the prototype of Julian Fichtner. It would depict his final, absolute loneliness—the result of his superficial relations with human beings, friends, and sweethearts. An important role would be assigned to one such friend, who may be looked upon as the forerunner of Stefan von Sala. The plot would probably end tragically.

That very year, 1900, Schnitzler, who was in the midst of his most productive period, and was working upon several literary projects at the same time, made note of another theme which he considered worthy of future dramatic treatment: The real father finds his son living with someone else whom the son regards as his father. In jealousy, he tells his son the truth. The son, however, loves his foster father so much that in order to prevent the disclosure of the true facts, he kills the intruding father.

Schnitzler, the subtle psychologist, immediately begins to question the motives of his characters. Why should this stranger break the family peace. Whence should arise, after the lapse of so many years, his sudden longing for his son? Of course, the stranger might feel himself despised by the insolent young man who is, perhaps, socially superior. The son might be a young count. The stranger might, therefore, retaliate by telling him: "I am your father." Schnitzler considers this possibility and rejects it as too trivial.

If, however, the stranger were the aging egoist whom Schnitzler had been considering as a possible hero for a play, if he were the bachelor who feels loneliness settling about him, would not his efforts to regain his lost offspring appear quite plausible; and would not the defeat of his efforts lend depth and pathos to his tragic fate?

In four successive outlines, during 1900 and 1901, Schnitzler attempts to combine the plot of the lonely bachelor with that of the son between two fathers. He is compelled by the nature of the material to create the bachelor father and the foster father as opposing types: the former as an unstable, irresponsible Bohemian, full of wit and fascination but devoid of moral sense; and the latter as an honest, good-natured individual following a definite, responsible calling. In Schnitzler's works these contrasting figures tend to take shape as the artist and the physician.

The central problem, which emerges more and more clearly in the course of successive outlines, is the following: Which father has a greater hold upon a son—a father who bases his claim upon ties of blood, or a father who nourishes, protects, and showers love upon his supposed offspring from infancy to manhood? In order that this main problem might be stripped of all extraneous considerations, the two fathers have to be shown at a time when they are both equally in need of the son's companionship and affection: on the one hand—Julian, the artist, who, at the end of a shiftless career with no longer any prospect of finding even a temporary haven in the arms of a mistress, seeks the son as his last bulwark against the chill of declining years; on the other hand—the dutiful physician, prototype of Professor Wegrath, who, bereaved of his wife and deserted by his hot-blooded daughter, seeks refuge from ill-deserved loneliness.

In the first place, the dramatic problem, therefore, demands the death of the physician's wife, Mrs. Wegrath of the final version; for this death, either before the curtain rises or else early in the course of action, supplies the necessary incentive moment. It leaves the husband more dependent upon the son, who must, henceforth, fill in the gap of affection. Furthermore, it removes Julian's last scruples and makes him feel that the hour has come to reveal everything to his child. In the second place, the dramatic problem demands the disappearance of Johanna, the physician's daughter. However, with whom could she elope? The most likely candidate for a girl's romantic infatuation in Vienna at the turn of the century would probably be an army officer. In the interest of dramatic economy, Schnitzler is compelled to reject this obvious possibility, for there is no need of introducing a new character when the author can make use of Julian's friend Sala, whose connection with the main plot is still undefined. But why should Johanna fall in love with Sala rather than with Julian or with someone younger than either? To motivate the love of the seventeen-year-old girl for the older Sala, Schnitzler has to present the latter under the shadow of death, so that his presence will exercise upon Johanna's imagination the same irresistible fascination that soldiers, about to leave for the front, exercise upon romantic maidens.

By resorting to the expedient of giving Sala a background of eternity, Schnitzler removes him beyond the pale of petty human follies. However, as soon as he introduces this new theme the love of a young girl for a man doomed to inevitable death—Schnitzler is creating a situation filled with such powerful emotional appeal that the center of interest immediately shifts from the original main characters to the minor characters, Sala and Johanna. Nor can Schnitzler wholly overcome this difficulty in succeeding versions. Sala is alive from the very moment that the dramatist conceives him in his imagination, while Julian, Felix, and Dr. Wegrath remain shadowy figures, in spite of all the labor devoted to them. One feels almost that the latter are puppets who have been created to illustrate a problem, and that they are nonexistent outside of the particular problem, whereas Sala, originally an unimportant figure but somehow endowed with the breath and fragrance of life, forces his way into importance, against the wishes perhaps even of his creator.

In order to prevent dramatic emphasis from being wholly diverted from the central problem and its solution, Schnitzler now seeks to develop subtler motivation for the acts and decisions of his principal characters, the son and the two fathers. He has to strengthen the links between son and foster father so as to offset, and more than offset, the biological bonds between the son and Julian. He does this, to some extent, by assigning to the son the same profession as that of the foster father. Both are physicians. Since the older man had been conceived as an honest, kindly, and diligent practitioner, the younger man must, by contrast, be depicted as one who is dissatisfied with mere practice, as one who seeks to adventure into original research and to devote himself primarily to the theory of medicine,—for in his veins flows the blood of the artist-adventurer Julian. Hence, in an outline of the second act early in 1901, Schnitzler includes the following notation: "The son has just come home from the clinic. He has reached a definite decision. He will give up his practice and devote himself entirely to theory. 'I shall never reach the point of seeing in human beings merely bed numbers. I suffer too much; that is my weakness. I suspect it is also my great strength. Yes, I'd remain a physician, if I had the power to kill.' 'We can comfort,' answers the father. 'What a pitiful thing—this lying to patients!'"

In a sketch of the play, written by Schnitzler in June, 1901, during a vacation in Salzburg and entitled *Jung-*

gesellen, the parts later played by Dr. Wegrath and Felix are assigned to Dr. Pflugfelder and his son Hans. Considerable space is devoted to the discussion of medical topics, such as the right to kill patients who are incurably sick, and the duty of physicians to lie when they can no longer save.

Now, Schnitzler had been planning, since 1899, a drama of the physician's calling, a drama which he did not complete until 1911 and which was later published under the title *Professor Bernhardi*. Toward the end of 1901 and early in 1902, Schnitzler finds himself occupied with two prospective dramas, the embryonic *Professor Bernhardi* and the nearly completed *Junggesellen*. The two plays have several themes in common and several similar characters. The possibility of combining the dramas inevitably occurs to him. He realizes that in some way a compelling motive must be found for the son's behavior in *Junggesellen*. Could not this motive be somehow connected with problems of the medical profession? The following suggestion appeals to him: "The son, for medical reasons, helps his mother commit suicide. His foster father, the practical physician, turns from him in horror. The bachelor (Julian) thinks that the time has come to assert his rights to his son. He reveals himself but is rejected."

During 1902 and the first few months of 1903, Schnitzler continues to work on a synthesis of both dramas. In the latter year he completes a combined version in five acts. This is now, for the first time, entitled *Der einsame Weg*. The dramatis personae are: Dr. Pflugfelder, Mrs. Pflugfelder, their son Hans, their daughter Johanna, Herr von Sala, Julian Werber, Professor Bernhardi, Irene Herms, Julian's servant, and a female attendant at the hospital.

Though Schnitzler afterwards rejects this version, and

though he relentlessly dissolves the temporary combination of both plays, nevertheless, the process of welding and severing leaves ineradicable traces upon the final draft. An analysis of this intermediate stage ought, therefore, to shed considerable light upon both dramas, and it ought perhaps to reveal, in addition, details of Schnitzler's view of life which failed to be included in the published version.

The first act takes place at the Pflugfelder home. Johanna is telling Sala about her sick mother and about the medical conference that is being held in the adjoining room between Professor Bernhardi, Dr. Pflugfelder, and the latter's son Hans, who is Bernhardi's clinical assistant. Sala mentions his prospective trip to Bactria with an archaeological expedition. He is interrupted by Professor Bernhardi and Hans, who have just completed their medical examination. After a few polite words of greeting, Sala and Johanna leave. And now, Hans learns from the specialist that all hope must be abandoned. Mrs. Pflugfelder cannot be cured. The conversation between the two physicians, which Schnitzler could not use in the final draft, shows his subtle insight into the human and moral problems of a profession which was originally his own. Medical discussions occupy the greater part of the first act. They give way, at the close of the act, to a happy family scene. Mrs. Pflugfelder is telling about her youth in Italy and about the scenes she would like to revisit after her recovery. She recalls her happy days as a singer. Twelve years have passed since her last charity concert. At that time Mrs. Sala was still alive, and Julian Werber was at the height of his fame. Memories of happy days gone by cast a golden autumnal haze over the scene. Mrs. Pflugfelder begins to sing a song of Cornelius. Before it is finished she becomes blind. The first act is thus brought to a very effective end. The second act, which takes place at the house of Julian Werber, resembles more closely the final printed version. It is filled with the egotist's complaint of increasing loneliness and the sorrows of old age. He learns from Sala that Mrs. Pflugfelder has just died very suddenly, and he feels that the hour has come when he can lay claim to Hans.

The third act reaches its climax in the scene in which Hans confesses that his mother begged him for poison to ease her suffering, and that he granted her request. Pflugfelder turns in horror from the matricide.

The fourth act, which resembles, in the main, the printed version, begins with the melancholy love scene between Johanna and Sala. Then follows the still sadder scene between Julian and Sala. Hans comes to offer Sala his services as physician to the Bactrian expedition, for he now realizes that he is not justified in shortening the life of a human being—not even of one incurably ill—and he wants to atone by exposing his own life to danger on a scientific mission. Julian, hoping to induce Hans to remain with him, determines to reveal himself to the latter.

The fifth act takes place at the hospital in the room of Hans, the clinical assistant. Julian reveals the secret of his relationship to Mrs. Pflugfelder, and tells of his need for his son's affection as a bulwark against the chill of old age. His remorse and his desire for atonement, however, come much too late. Hans feels that now, more than ever before, his place is with his foster father. He thinks that a person has done very little for a child, if he has merely brought it into the world. He believes that he must devote himself to the man who, though under no moral obligation, has yet provided during so many years for his comfort and happiness. Especially would it be wrong to desert the much-tried physician, now that Mrs. Pflugfelder is dead, and now that Johanna has committed suicide because of her hopeless love for the doomed Sala. However, when Pflugfelder learns of his son's intention to remain with him, he refuses to accept this sacrifice and counsels Hans with the words: "I do not want you to change your original plans. Your seeking danger means that you desire to atone. Name it what you will—fate, chance, God—whatever power there is above us, let it pass judgment on your life. Perhaps you were right in doing what you did. Perhaps you are one of those to whom our old standards do not apply—one of those who may do what others may not. If you come back alive, I shall believe this to be the case."

When the curtain falls upon the last act, and sentence has been passed upon the leading characters of the play, Schnitzler finds that he has, perhaps, succeeded in solving a problem but that it certainly is not the one which he originally set out to solve. In an effort to balance the "Sala-Johanna" scenes, he has been compelled to place greater emphasis, upon the scenes between father and son. Furthermore, in seeking to better motivate the son's behavior, he has seized upon the drastic expedient of making the son the murderer of his mother. The inevitable result following the introduction of this sensational theme was a shifting of the center of interest from the original problem, that of the son between two fathers, to a wholly new problem, that of the right of a physician to kill a patient incurably ill. Moreover, the autumnal, Bohemian atmosphere of *Junggesellen*—the drama that originally concentrated on the fate of Julian and Sala—was so far removed from the robust, scientific atmosphere of Professor Bernhardi's clinic that the synthetic version failed to convince, or to produce that illusion of reality which is essential to all good art.

And now, what is there for Schnitzler to do? Obviously, the incompatible themes that had been welded together must again be severed, and the synthetic drama must be resolved into its component parts. This might best be accomplished by concentrating one play solely on the fate of Julian, his loneliness, his old age, and his relation to his son; and by constructing a second play about problems of the physician's calling, with Professor Bernhardi and the Pflugfelders as central figures.

During a vacation at Lugano in May, 1903, Schnitzler outlines two such dramas. The first he entitles *Egoisten*, and the second, *Verurteilte*. In separating his material, the dramatist discovers that his chief difficulty lies in the "Sala" episodes. On the one hand, Sala, the aging egoist, is a fit companion for Julian. His calm acceptance of his tragic destiny brings into greater relief the folly of Julian's sentimental whining. On the other hand, as a person doomed to death because of incurable illness, Sala seems no less important for the psycho-medical discussions than Mrs. Pflugfelder.

Schnitzler is at first tempted to treat Sala from the latter angle. According to the earliest outline of *Verurteilte*, this drama is to differ from the synthetic version chiefly in the omission of the "Julian" material. It is to retain the "Sala-Johanna" scenes. A second and more detailed outline, however, fails to mention Sala. Schnitzler, apparently, soon realized that any medical discussions that might center about the doomed Sala could be appended equally well to the case of the doomed Mrs. Pflugfelder. Furthermore, should a love story be necessary to relieve the reader from too much preoccupation with professional themes, such relief could be better afforded by a younger man, perhaps a son of Bernhardi, than by the somber Sala. The latter could thus be restored to his original role as Julian's partner. In the six outlines of *Egoisten*, preserved among Schnitzler's manuscripts, we can trace the gradual changes that developed in the drama, throughout the spring and summer of 1903, until its final emergence under the title *Der einsame Weg*. Since Dr. Pflugfelder had to be kept in reserve for another play, a new foster father must be called in to fill the vacancy. He is found in Wegrath—a professor at the art academy, an official who takes his responsibilities seriously, a person who knows his limitations and therefore lays no claim to genius, a skilled painter who completes his annual picture for the exhibition without depending upon inspiration or changing moods. In the opinion of his adversary, the erratic Julian, Wegrath belongs to that group of people whose destiny it is to follow the path of duty blindly, unaware of the rainbow colors about them. "It is their lot to receive in their arms beings who are tired or broken from some passionate experience. But they never know whence these come. It is granted to them, also, to raise up and cherish other beings. But they never understand whither these disappear. They exist in order to sacrifice themselves unconsciously and to find in such sacrifice a happiness which would seem rather pitiable to others."

Wegrath realizes, no less than Julian or Sala, that all the ways on which we wander end in solitude. He, too, is oppressed by the consciousness of the apparent meaninglessness of existence. In work, however, he has found a means of drugging this consciousness. "Work is, after all, the only thing that helps one to overcome the feeling of loneliness," he tells Julian. He has no illusions about children or friends. No one can share his deepest experiences. "There is so much that calls, and lures, and tears young people away from us from the very beginning. We struggle for the possession of our children from the moment they are born but without any real hope of victory. That is the course of the world: they cannot belong to us. And, as for other human beings, our friends, too, are only guests in our lives: they get up from the table when the meal is over; they go down the steps; they, like us, have their own way and their own affairs. It's all quite natural."

The only person in whom Wegrath has absolute faith is his wife. And yet, though he has lived for more than two decades at her side, he really does not share in her inner life. He never learns of her experience with Julian. When she feels the need of confiding to someone, it is not to him that she turns but rather to her family physician, Dr. Reumann. The physician finds words of comfort which the husband could never have found. For Wegrath, who never did wrong and, hence, never had to forgive himself, could not possibly interpret correctly the failings of others. He would be merely stunned and bewildered, if his eyes were suddenly opened to the complexity of the relations between the human beings about him. But the physician understands. In him there is something of Ibsen's Dr. Rank, something of Sudermann's Pastor Heffterdingk, and something of his creator, Schnitzler, himself. Temperamentally so constituted as to remain throughout life a decent respectable citizen, Dr. Reumann secretly envies those beings who have the talent and the will power to be rogues, hypocrites, seducers, and unscrupulous cynics. He cannot condemn, since he has peered beneath the surface of things. He calms Mrs. Wegrath by assuring her that she has no cause for self-reproach. Far better than the negative virtue of innocence is the positive one of making others happy. In years of sacrifice she has more than atoned for the error of her youth. When she asks whether one has a right to let a son go through life without knowing to whom he owes his existence, Dr. Reumann wisely replies: "We don't want to make any generalizations, because in that way the clearest things become blurred. But I personally believe that a lie which has proved so strong that it can support the peace of a family is, at least, as worthy of reverence as a truth which can do nothing except destroy the picture of the past, cloud the feeling of the present, and confuse the outlook of the future."

Similar words are uttered by the person most vitally affected, young Felix Wegrath, who is substituted for Hans Pflugfelder in the final version. From Julian he learns the truth of his origin, but this truth is devoid of meaning for him. "I cannot bring myself to see, before me, deceivers and deceived where an hour ago I saw these persons, so dear to me, in pure relations to each other. It is, furthermore, impossible for me to feel myself another being from the one I have been hitherto. It is a truth without significance. A vivid dream would be more compelling than this tale that you have told me of days gone by. Nothing has changed— nothing. The memory of my mother is no less sacred to me than it was before. And the man in whose house I was born and reared, who surrounded my childhood and youth with tenderness and care, and who loved my mother, means just as much to me now as he did before—almost, in fact, more."

Felix, the army officer and the representative of active youth, has little sympathy for decadent aesthetes. He belongs to the new generation that faces duties without fear, and without overmuch deliberation. The earlier generation, of Julian and Sala, has shunned responsibilities, avoided hard work, and, unperturbed by the morrow, has thought only of extracting from each moment its full quota of pleasures and nervous stimuli. "You who live on, cease to weep; and make the most of your day," is the cardinal principle of its faith. Julian has followed this principle. In the intoxication of earlier and more glorious years, he led a young girl astray—probably one of several. When the hour came for him to elope with her, fear of the consequences overwhelmed him. To link another person's fate to his meant depriving himself of freedom, foregoing the splendor of beckoning adventures, and ultimately submitting to dreary Philistinism. He, therefore, fled alone, unscrupulous about leaving behind him the girl who had entrusted her body and soul to him, and cruelly putting out of his mind all thoughts of the child to be born to him. But the promising decades have passed, and the infinite possibilities that once enticed him are shorn of their glamor. In vain does he turn then to the son whom he formerly neglected. Felix remains cold and unmoved, a stranger to the man who gave him being.

In a scene, omitted in the final version, Julian's last mistress comes to take leave of him. Though she is still fond of him, nevertheless, she feels that at twenty-six she ought not to refuse the marriage proposal of a young horse-trader. Julian is left to face old age without a single human being for whom his life can still hold significance.

Julian's plaints of inescapable loneliness are especially bitter in his conversations with Sala, in whom he senses an allied spirit. "Is naught to remain of all the glow with which I embraced the world save a sort of foolish anger that it's all over?" he asks his companion. And the wiser Sala reminds him that all efforts to evade loneliness must remain futile. "You dread being alone? And if you had a wife at your side, would you be any less lonely today? And if children and grandchildren lived near you, would you not be alone? And if you had retained your wealth, your fame, your genius, would you not still be alone? And if a train of bacchantes were to accompany us . . . the last road, we all travel alone, we who have never belonged to anyone." The loneliness of old age is the egoist's just punishment. Never having given of himself to others, he ought not to expect any returns. Friendship to him has been merely a device for exchanging jokes. Love to him has meant being loved. Too late does he learn that real happiness lies in giving and not in taking, and that escape from misery lies in resigned acceptance of one's fate whatever it may be.

The sweet weariness of autumn hangs over the whole play. The golden leaves are ever falling; the air is continually filled with vanishing memories of faded splendor; and youth, as well as age, is enticed by the soft melody of resignation. There is even a twilight haze about the only important love scene of the play—a scene dear to the heart of its author and very touching in its tender sadness—the scene between Johanna and Sala in the garden of the latter's villa. Johanna knows that Sala is doomed, though this knowledge has still been kept from him. Each word with its mellow tone adds to the loveliness of the dialogue:

Johanna. Do you know what I imagine? . . . That today is our day—that it belongs to us, and to us only. We called for this day; and if we wished, we could hold on to it . . . Today all other people live on earth only as guests. Isn't that so? . . . I suppose it's because you once spoke of this day.

Sala. Of this—

Johanna. Yes . . . when my mother was still alive. And now the day has really come. The leaves are red, the golden mist lies over the forests, the sky is pale and distant; and the day is even more beautiful and sad than I ever dreamed it could be. And I experience the day in your garden and mirror myself in your pond. (*She stands then and looks down.*) And yet, we shall not be able to hold on to this day, this golden day, any more than the water can retain my image when I go away.

Sala. It is strange, but in this clear, warm air there is already a foreboding of winter and snow.

Johanna. What does it matter to you? When this foreboding will have become a reality, you will long since have entered upon a new spring.

Sala. What do you mean?

Johanna. Well, the place to which you're going has no winter that can compare with ours.

Sala. (*Brooding.*) No; no winter comparable to ours. (*Pause.*) And you?

Johanna. I?

Sala. I mean—when I'm away, what will you do?

Johanna. When you're away? (*She looks at him. He gazes into the distance.*) Were you not long away from me? And in the last analysis, are you not far away even at this moment?

Sala. What are you saying? I *am* with you . . . What will you do, Johanna?

Johanna. Why, I've already told you. I'll go away, just as you are going. (*Sala shakes his head.*)

Johanna. As soon as possible. Now, while I still have the courage. Who knows what would become of me afterwards, if I should stay here?

Sala. As long as one is young, all doors are open; and at every door, the world begins.

Johanna. Yes, the world is wide, and heaven is infinite; but only so long as we're not attached to anybody. And that's why I want to go away.

Sala. "Away"—that's easily said. But, to do so, you must make all sorts of preparations, and you must have some plan or other. You utter the word as though you had merely to put on wings in order to fly far away.

Johanna. Determination is the equivalent of wings.

Sala. Are you not afraid, Johanna?

Johanna. Longing without fear would be pretty cheap longing; we'd hardly be worthy of that sort.

Sala. To where will this longing lead you?

Johanna. I'll find my way.

Sala. You can choose your way, but not the people you'll encounter.

Johanna. Do you think I don't know that I may be destined to experience more than just the beautiful? I shall face ugliness and meanness.

Sala. And how will you endure it? . . . Will you be able to endure it?

Johanna. I shall not always be truthful, as I am toward you. I shall lie, and I am glad at the thought. I shall not always be happy, and not always wise. I shall make mistakes and suffer. I suppose that's probably necessary.

Sala. You know all this beforehand, and yet? . . .

Johanna. Yes.

Sala. And why? . . . Why are you going away, Johanna?

Johanna. Why am I going? . . . I want some day to have to shudder before myself as only that person can to whom nothing is any longer strange—to shudder as you must have to shudder when you look back upon your life. Isn't that so?

Sala. Yes, sometimes. But, then, in such moments of shuddering there is really no looking back. All is again the present. And the present is past. (*He sits down on the bench.*)

Johanna. What do you mean?

(*Sala with his hand before his eyes, is silent.*)

Johanna. What is the matter? Where are you? (*Gentle rustling of wind, and falling of leaves.*)

Sala. I am a child riding on a pony over a field. My father, who is behind me, calls. There at the window my mother is calling; she has a gray silk shawl about her dark hair and beckons to me . . . All that—all that is with me, if only I close my eyes. And it is nearer to me than you, Johanna, if my eyes are not fixed upon you, and if you are silent.

(*Johanna has turned her melancholy eyes upon him.*)

Sala. "Present" . . . what does that really mean? Do we stand on the same footing with the present as with a friend whom we embrace breast to breast—or as with a foe who hounds us? Is not the word that has just resounded already a memory? Is not the tone with which a melody begins, a memory even before the song has ended? Isn't your entrance into this garden a memory, Johanna? Isn't the walk you took through the meadow yonder as much a memory as the walk of beings who died long ago.

Johanna. No, it shouldn't be so. That thought makes me sad.

Sala. (*Returning again to the present.*) Why? It shouldn't make you sad, Johanna. It is in just such hours that we realize we have lost nothing—that we really can't lose anything.

Johanna. Oh, if only you had forgotten it all, lost it all, and I could be everything to you!

Sala. (*Almost surprised.*) Johanna—

Johanna. (*Passionately.*) I love you*! (Pause.)*

Sala. In a few days I'll be gone, Johanna. You know it . . . you have known it.

Johanna. I know it. Why do you repeat it? Do you think, perhaps, that I want all of a sudden to hang on to you like an infatuated creature and to dream of eternity? No, that's not my way. O no! . . . But I did want to tell you just once that I love you. You'll let me say it once, won't you? Do you hear? I love you. And I should like for you to hear it again some day just as I'm saying it now—in some other moment as beautiful as this one . . . at a time when neither of us shall know the other any more.

Sala. Truly, Johanna, you may be sure of this. The tone of your voice will never escape me. But why speak of a final parting? We'll see each other again later . . . perhaps, in three years . . . or in five . . . (*Smiling.*) And by then you will probably have become a princess; and I, the ruler of a sunken town . . . Why are you silent?

In scenes, such as this one, Schnitzler takes his rank among the masters of literature. Here he is not merely a skeptical scientist who uses art as a means of dissecting human emotions and human relations, just as in his early days he used his medical knowledge to diagnose human bodies and their ills—here he is a poet by the grace of God.

Our genetic study of his play enables us to shed some light on his method of composition, and to reveal the framework of his final product. We can observe him weaving his patterns of thought carefully and logically. We can see him impelled, by his material and by his mental habits, toward certain conclusions. However, the magic touch with which he converts the ore of his subject matter into the pure gold of art eludes us, and must always elude us. The color, light, fragrance, atmosphere, depth, and peculiar sweetness of his themes are beyond analysis, and they must remain so. For these are phenomena that have their roots elsewhere than in the writer's consciousness—phenomena that at times well up to the surface, and then recede; phenomena that interpenetrate word symbols, and enable them to move the heart and fire the imagination. And here our genetic method of interpretation must fail us. Here, face to face with the unlocked secret of the artist, all scientific and pseudo-scientific investigations reach their limit; we are forced to seek refuge in the mystic word "inspiration," in order to explain our incapacity for further explanation. In fortunate moments Schnitzler is inspired, and it is then that he wields the scepter of a great artist. In such moments he takes his place easily in the foremost ranks of contemporary literary masters.

CHAPTER VII

THE CALL OF LIFE

HAS a physician the right to kill a patient, incurably ill, in order to ease the latter's suffering? This question occupied Schnitzler's attention while he was working on *Der einsame Weg*. At one time he thought even of assigning to this problem as much weight as he had to the other main themes of the drama. Hans Pflugfelder was to assert the physician's right to administer poison under certain circumstances, and Professor Bernhardi was to deny this right. In the end Hans was to realize his error, and then to seek atonement. It was only after much hesitation and experimentation that Schnitzler finally decided to exclude from the published version a consideration of this problem, in order not to overburden the dramatic action with too complicated and too diversified material.

After the appearance of *Der einsame Weg* in 1903, Schnitzler's mind reverted to this excluded theme and its dramatic possibilities. He began to see it not merely as a physician's problem but also as a general human problem: May one kill a person who is incurably ill?

Schnitzler tried to picture a situation in which a problem of this kind might actually arise. Suppose that a father were ill for many years without any hope of recovery and that his daughter were compelled to nurse him throughout all this period, while her youth flitted away careworn and loveless, could we not understand there welling up in the heart of such a daughter a wish that the death of the patient might be hastened? And if, in an hour of temptation, or in a feverish state of mind induced by overlong vigil at the side of the sick man, this wish were converted into an act, should we assert that her deed is beyond forgiveness?

Since our normal judgment revolts against such an act, the dramatist, who was trying to arouse our sympathy for the murderess, would have to present the patient in the worst possible light and the young girl under the strongest possible stress. He would have to depict the father as cruel, cowardly, violent, and unjust. He would have to portray the daughter as lonely and worn-out, enduring privations patiently, earning abuse instead of gratitude, and yet submitting without a murmur to every whim of her exacting parent. He would then have to show life in its most enticing form, as spring and love and youth flash past the sick chamber to which she is chained by a merciless tyrant. The girl, caught between the lure of life and the call of duty, might under these circumstances respond to the former without wholly losing our sympathy.

The first outline of *Der Ruf des Lebens*, preserved among Schnitzler's literary remains, reveals his intention to center this drama about such a situation: "A young girl sits every evening at the bedside of her father, who has been ill for years. Without is the spring night. The girl is apathetic, worn-out; she almost hates the dying person; perhaps she yearns for his death. Her life: her mother died two years ago; her father is wrathful, niggardly, almost deaf, and he never has a kind word for her. She can hardly ever leave the house any more. If she does, he abuses her. In former years she at least could visit her cousin and take walks with her mother. But that, too, has ceased. She and her father have to live on a scanty pension in an old house in Nagler

Street. Only once during the winter has she left the house; she has had to atone for it bitterly. Uncle, aunt, and cousin took her with them to a ball. There she made the acquaintance of a young physician, who fascinated her. He lives at the hospital. He has told her: 'Come to me, I'll always wait for you.' She has seen him go past her door several times since. How long will the present situation last? Today the doctor said that it would be a godsend to the patient if he were suddenly to die. She knows that the doctor gives him morphium injections. Her father moans; he asks for morphium. She gives him more than he demands, and he dies. When she sees him lying there dead, she feels no sorrow nor remorse. At last the realization comes to her: 'I am free! I can do as I wish.' Perhaps she has had hardly any sleep for days, and is in a feverish state. What good does it do him if she remains sitting here? It is almost midnight. What is she to do? She wants to get out into the open. She hurries through the streets. She feels a great longing for human beings; hence, naturally, she wishes to be with the physician. She hurries to the hospital. She rings the bell, and inquires for the physician's apartment. The door is pointed out to her. She knocks. She doesn't realize what she is doing. When the physician opens the door, she can say only: 'My father . . . ' The young physician goes out with her. Silently they walk through the night. They come to her house. They go up the steps. She opens the door. The physician enters with her. The physician exclaims: 'Why, he is dead !' She says: 'I murdered him.' The physician doubts her sanity. She insists that he believe her. She tells him the whole truth. She also tells him why she did it. He looks at her; she seems quite different from the careworn, almost ugly person whom he met at the ball.

Perhaps he can hardly recall her. He tells her that he is engaged. They watch throughout the night beside the corpse . . . They talk the matter over fully."

According to this outline, the key to the drama is to be sought in the dialogue between the daughter and the physician at the beside of the dead father. The physician would probably neither wholly justify nor totally condemn her deed. He would rather try to understand the state of mind that led her to such a point of despair. She would soon realize that her act did not bring her any nearer to happiness, but that, on the contrary, it saddled her conscience with a knowledge of sin and guilt. The physician would calm her upset nerves and would appease her remorse. He would lay all blame on the irresistible call of life. The dialogue would probably end in Schnitzler's usual fatalistic note: There are no saints, and there are no sinners. There are no angelic daughters, and there are no wicked murderesses.

The whole play might even be reduced to discussions between the two characters from the moment the girl enters the doctor's room in the hospital until the end of the bedside scene. Schnitzler's physician is usually, also, a psychoanalyst. He regards it as an important duty of his profession to restore sick souls as well as sick bodies to health. He does not upbraid patients but studies each individual in order to discover the best way to comfort and to cure.

Now, the more the wisdom, the finer the tact, and the greater the tolerance which Schnitzler assigns to the physician, the less intelligible does the crime of the daughter become. We doubt whether it was necessary for the girl to step over a corpse in order to reach out for the physician's love. We wonder whether a calm sage, even if he is not advanced in years, best symbolizes to a young girl the lure of adventure, mystery, and life.

Schnitzler early recognized these difficulties; and in an outline of March 29, 1905, he modified the plot by leaving to the physician merely the function of confessor, consoler, and *raisonneur*, and by bestowing upon a new character, an army lieutenant, the dashing qualities that would fascinate an impressionable maiden.

Having projected this new character into the drama, Schnitzler must strengthen the glamor which surrounds him to such an intensity that even a crime would not appear too high a price to pay for his love. This can best be effected, as Schnitzler had shown in *Der Schleier der Beatrice* and in *Der einsame Weg*, by placing the hero under the shadow of death.

With love and death and fate as fundamental chords, Schnitzler has the stage set for a stirring drama. The first act opens very effectively: A war has broken out. The troops are to leave for the front. Lieutenant Max will be in the foremost line of battle. He will surely not return alive. It is his last day of freedom, his last day in town. Marie Moser sits at the window watching the soldiers march past. She is chained to a sick father, who tyrannizes her. She thinks longingly of the one evening throughout the long winter when she left her home and attended a ball with her young cousin, Katharina. There she met the officer Max, who aroused her to love. But now the months are passing. She feels her youth wither away, while her seventy-nine-year-old father jeers: "You are twenty-six. Time enough. Time enough. Twenty-six, and young, and beautiful, and a woman with white skin and round arms. Nothing lost yet. Have patience. And if I become ninety, then you are only thirty-seven—still time enough for all the fun you want." Marie yearns to escape from the dull, petty, and morbid atmosphere of the sick chamber. Such an opportunity is offered her by a forester, who wants to marry her and to take her with him to his peaceful country home. She is, however, not yet sufficiently matured by experience to accept this offer and to resign herself to a quiet, unsensational existence. Throughout the long winter evenings she has recalled many times the image of the lieutenant whom she has seen but once, when she danced with him in a brightly lighted hall, and, yet, for whom she would be willing to sacrifice honor, life, and salvation. He has waited for her since the ball. But she has not come, because her strength of purpose had been sapped by the demands of her exacting father. Now that she is ready to answer the call of life, even though it may lead to sin, she fears that it is too late. From her cousin, Katharina, she learns that the squadron to which Max is attached will not leave for the front until the morrow. The night is still hers. Now she finds the courage to free herself. When her father asks for a sleeping potion, she gives him enough for a hundred nights; and, as he collapses, she dashes forth into life, love, and the mystery of the unknown.

This powerful opening act is followed by an almost melodramatic second act which takes place in the room of Lieutenant Max on the evening before setting out for the front. With subtle irony, Schnitzler spins out the threads of his story until he has enmeshed every one of his characters in the labyrinth of fate. To him each happening is the result of a multiplicity of causes and the beginning of innumerable, unpredictable consequences. He, therefore, sees fit to link the relation of Marie to her father with the tragic death of an entire regiment, of whose existence they are barely aware.

The officers of the regiment to which Max is attached have requested that they be assigned to the most dangerous position in the coming battle. They have pledged a solemn oath not to return alive. They want their heroic sacrifice to wipe out a legendary stain on their regimental flag. They want to atone, with their blood, for the flight of their predecessors during a decisive military encounter thirty years before. But their request would not have been made had it not been for their colonel, whose suggestion revived the almost forgotten legend of the flight. The old colonel might not have offered this suggestion had he not been married to a young wife who betrayed him for one of the officers. Not knowing which officer to suspect, he had determined to send the whole regiment to certain death, in order to punish the guilty person. But this guilty officer is Max, who might not have entered into the affair with the colonel's wife, if Marie had answered the call of life earlier. Marie would have come to him and would have preserved him from his perilous step, if she had not been forced to spend every evening at the side of her sick father. And this father was the very person whose example brought on the original flight of the regiment and the loss of the campaign thirty years before.

Where does the chain of cause and effect begin, and where does it end? Is old Moser the person chiefly responsible for the present sacrifice of the young men? Or is it Marie who has doomed the regiment, because she remained a dutiful daughter too long? Or is it the lieutenant, because he has succumbed to the wiles of a woman unhappily married? Or is it the colonel, because his wife has betrayed him? Or shall we reject all of these causes, and accept at full value the confession of the colonel that he was merely tired of inactivity and sham maneuvers, that he wanted to make sure his regiment would be on the firing line, and that he used the legend of the flight solely as a good excuse for getting them there. "There is no doctor who will for thirty years attend at the bedside of dolls instead of patients, nor any lawyer who will practice his art on camouflaged criminals. Even pastors often preach before people who really believe in heaven and hell. But I was forced to convert my profession into a game. Heavens! I don't know what I would have done, if the war had not finally come. However, I don't trust fate; and, since there are regiments that never come under fire, I have taken measures to prevent the whole thing from being, again, simply a farce."

What really determines a happening? Perhaps it is the sum total of all events that preceded since the birth of time. Hence, properly interpreted, nothing we do, or leave undone, is unimportant. In a parable, entitled *Die dreifache Warnung* and published in 1911, Schnitzler tells of a vigorous and healthy young man who sets out on a journey. On entering a forest, he hears a voice warning him not to continue unless he wishes to commit murder. He refuses to be frightened, and hastens through the forest. Emerging upon a meadow, he again hears a voice warning him not to cross the field unless he wishes to bring destruction upon his country. Disregarding this admonition, he strides on until he comes to a steep cliff. Again a voice charges him to halt unless he wants to die. He climbs boldly, however, until sundown, when he reaches the top. There he boasts of his success in defying all warnings. "No murder weighs upon my soul; my beloved country slumbers undisturbed below; and I live." But soon he learns, to his dismay, that he was too rash in drawing his conclusions. While passing through the forest, he stepped on a worm, and thus killed a living thing, whose destiny in the stream of becoming and being was thereby unfulfilled. In walking through the meadow, he brushed aside a butterfly, and thus changed the direction of its flight. It fluttered on until it reached the royal park. From its larvae will spring, during the following year, a caterpillar which will one day rouse the queen from her slumber so suddenly that her heart will be paralyzed with fear, and the fruit of her womb will perish. As a result, the brother of the king will inherit the throne and bring war and desolation upon the kingdom. The third prophecy, too, does not long remain unfulfilled, because the youth in the darkness of night cannot descend from the cliff without fatal injury. Before dying, he calls upon the mysterious power to reveal itself; and the answer comes: "No mortal has yet recognized me. My names are many. The superstitious call me fate; the fools, chance; and the pious, God. To those who think themselves wise, I am the force which was at the beginning of time and which manifests itself in all happenings unto eternity." "Then I curse you with my last breath," exclaims the youth, "for, if you are the force which was at the beginning of time and which manifests itself in all happenings unto eternity, then all this had to come about as it did: I had to stride through the forest in order to commit a murder; I had to wander over the meadow in order to bring ruin to my country; I had to climb the cliff in order to die. And all this was destined to happen in spite of your warning. Why was I, therefore, condemned to hear thrice this warning, which could not be of any use to me after all? Did this, too, have to happen? And why, O mockery of mockeries, do I with my last breath have to moan to you my helpless Why?"

Schnitzler insists that everything we do has significance. Vast cataclysms may spring from trivial beginnings. National tragedies may often be necessary in order to change the humble fortune of a humble being. The dynamic personality is, perhaps, merely a magnificent fool. The real hero is passive. His divine gift is the gift of understanding. He has insight into the complex relations about him. He sees events happening because they must happen, and he never condemns or waxes over-enthusiastic. No matter how commonplace they may seem to the ignorant, these events are, moreover, no less charged with magic than the breathtaking dreams of fairyland. A peaceful walk along a country lane with open eyes and discerning ears may stir a person more deeply than the most sensational adventures for which he may yearn. This wisdom does not, however, normally come to one until after one has waded through the foam of so-called "grand" experiences.

In *Der Ruf des Lebens*, Schnitzler, therefore, leads Marie through a weird series of adventures so as to make her ripe for the simple existence which he ultimately allots to her. She, who committed a crime in order to answer the lure of love, arrives at the quarters of her lieutenant shortly before he enters. When she sees that he is accompanied by someone, she conceals herself behind a curtain. The person is Irene, the colonel's wife. From her hiding place Marie becomes a witness of all that follows. Max rebukes Irene for persisting in tempting him. He recalls that the suspicious husband has just spoken to him as to a friend, urging him to tell the truth; but he has remained silent, and has thus deceived the understanding and forgiving old man. Irene enlightens him concerning the true character of her husband, a tolerant egoist who might be compared to Stefan von Sala, in *Der einsame Weg*. "You were as little his friend as ever I was his wife. Never has a person meant anything to him. You think, we're living with him under sun and stars; and, yet, we're nothing to him except partners at the same gambling table." She urges Max to flee with her and not to die at the front just to satisfy a mere whim of her husband. Their conversation is suddenly interrupted by the colonel, who has jumped in through a window. He shoots Irene, and commands Max to assume responsibility for the murder and to kill himself. As the colonel leaves and Max reaches out for a pistol, Marie steps from behind the curtain and almost throws herself into his arms. When Max reminds her that he must put an end to himself before dawn, her only answer is: "I have come." Over the body of the dead Irene, they rush forth into a night of love.

After this rapid succession of sensational scenes, Schnitzler experienced unusual difficulty in planning the final act. Having reached a climax of intensity, he could not resort to still shriller tones for the conclusion. Nor could he seriously consider ending the play with Marie's death or with her punishment by the State, since these forms of atonement were incompatible with the problem as viewed by a dramatist who sought to understand rather than to condemn human behavior. It was obvious to him that the final act would have to deal with Marie's efforts at readjusting herself to normal existence after the sweet and terrible night. This would be possible only if her crime were not made known. In the outline of March 29, 1905, Schnitzler has Marie return home before dawn. When the physician arrives, he finds her broken by the night's experiences. Though recognizing at a glance what has happened since

his last visit, he, nevertheless, feels that his first duty is to comfort the living: "Have no regrets. There are beings who have but a few hours time in which to live. You would have real cause for regret, if you had not enjoyed those hours."
This sentiment forms the keynote of successive versions with which Schnitzler experimented. The first version, preserved among his manuscripts, ends with Marie's realization that a quiet existence at the side of the kind physician is preferable to all the glamor of exciting adventures. A somewhat modified version, designated by the dramatist in his notes as *Fassung 1 b*, substitutes the forester for the physician. It ends with the forester's conciliatory words: "Your dreams filled me with shudders. But now that you have lived through them, I no longer shudder. Unfulfilled wishes glide through our souls like ghosts of remorse. But, what we have experienced, and experienced without regret, never comes back from the grave."
In a version of September, 1905, Marie does not return until days later. She imagines that the authorities are pursuing her, and she seeks refuge with the physician. He removes her fears by assuring her that her father's death was regarded everywhere as the result of natural causes. After a moment of relief, remorse again assails her. What if no one knows? Is she not still a parricide? Did she not kill, because life lured her on? And was this life worth the price? "I have peered into lies, and cowardice, and murder. I gave myself to a man to whom I signified nothing more than the lust of a final night. I wanted to die with him, but, in the great hour, he drove me away. Then I wanted to die alone. What more was there left for me? But morning came, and with it the sun, and the bright light. 'One more day,' I said, 'no longer.' I wandered on. And again came night.

I slept in the forest. Then fear came upon me. By now my crime must be discovered. They're looking for me. And I determined to put an end to myself, as soon as danger neared. But nobody took any interest in me; everyone spoke only of war. I recovered my senses. I heard people speak; I had some money with me; I could eat and sleep at the inn. And another day came. Again it was beautiful: the sun above me, wafting fields, forests, meadows. The longer I delayed, the harder it was to die. The memory of my beloved and of that night grew more and more dim. I began to think more about myself. I gave myself ever new respites: just to see the sun another day, to breathe one day more. I could hardly recall any longer what I had done. And something drew me here. As I came ever nearer to this place, I made up my mind: 'I will see this place once again, and then I will put an end to myself.' I no longer wanted to escape—not even when I entered here. But, when I saw you, my first words were: 'Save me!' Now I realize that this cry came from the depths of my soul. Now I know that throughout the days of my wanderings, I gave hardly any thought to my recent experiences. I have come from one murder; I have witnessed another murder; the person whom I loved has died . . . Why have I committed murder, if all this means so little that I hardly think of it now? What sort of creature am I to live on after all this?"

Marie's troubled question is best answered by the physician in the final scene of the third, or published, version. Time is hailed as the surest cure for all mental anguish. As long as the sun shines, and one is young, there is no reason to despair. Marie need not regard herself as a sinner. Should she, however, feel a desire for atonement, then let her submit to danger by offering her services as a nurse at the front. "Who knows—at some time in the future, on just such a day as this, the call of life may, perhaps, resound in your soul purer and deeper than it did on that other day when you experienced things that have such terrible and glowing names as 'murder' and 'love.'" Guilt and innocence, sin and virtue, evil and good are but words that have no permanent significance. The one thing which is certain is that some people are alive, while others are reposing under the ground. Let those who live on, therefore, cease to moan and to darken with cares their all too few days on earth.

This mild conclusion again emphasizes Schnitzler's tolerant passiveness. It again stresses the futility of all efforts to compel fate to do one's bidding, and the wisdom of calmly accepting our destiny, whatever it may be, without attempting to pass judgment upon it. For a time Schnitzler must have been satisfied with this conclusion, since he incorporated it in the published version, which appeared at the close of 1905. Soon thereafter doubts must have arisen in his mind as to the effectiveness of this ending. He must have become conscious of the fact that the complete lack of dramatic action in the final scenes was not wholly an asset. He must have felt the incongruity of having the colonel cold-bloodedly shoot down his wife a few minutes after preaching to Max the doctrine of understanding. Hence, in February, 1908, Schnitzler undertook a revision of the last two acts, beginning with the moment at which the colonel surprises the couple. In this revised version, the colonel contents himself with unmasking the lovers. He is not the deceived husband, because he foresaw that at some time his young wife would become faithless. He is merely hurt because the officer from whom he expected the truth withheld it from him. He, therefore, relieves Max from the command of the squadron, and appoints Lieutenant Albrecht as his successor. Max, who feels that he ought not to survive this disgrace, is persuaded by Albrecht to refrain from suicide and to re-enlist as a volunteer in order to meet a more glorious end in battle.

The scene then shifts to early dawn. The troops are preparing to march. Marie and Max, who have spent the last hours together, must take leave of each other. Though Marie wants to join him in death, Max refuses to listen to her. He insists that they have nothing in common save a single night together. Each being treads his own path and experiences his own fate. She may live on, in spite of her guilt, while he must die. The whole world is hers, while only a brief and gruesome hour is his.

A revised third act that was to take place behind the battle lines was sketched by Schnitzler, but was not completed. His purpose in this revision was, apparently, to stress still further the inscrutable ways of life. We may know the path we enter upon, but we cannot know to where it will ultimately lead us. Schnitzler, therefore, piled sensation upon sensation in an effort to show his characters as helpless pawns in the grip of forces beyond their control. Soon, however, he must have realized the futility of complicating the bewildering action still more. Though not wholly satisfied with the printed conclusion, he gave up, for the time, further attempts at revision; and he directed his attention to another play which was to illustrate even more clearly his doctrine that the soul is a vast and still insufficiently explored panorama. This play appeared in 1908 under the title *Das weite Land*.

CHAPTER VIII

THE PANORAMA OF THE SOUL

SCHNITZLER is the eternal questioner, the eternal doubter; and it is fundamental assumptions that he questions, and deeply ingrained beliefs upon which he casts doubt. For example, it is almost axiomatic that no person has the right to take the life of another. But, asks Schnitzler, how about a physician who is requested by a patient, incurably ill, to ease his suffering by administering poison to him? Does the above axiom still apply? *Der einsame Weg* and *Der Ruf des Lebens* sought to answer this question. Or, to use another illustration, it is a universal assumption on the part of husbands that their wives ought to be faithful to them. Schnitzler asks whether there are not some situations in life in which even this assumption would not necessarily hold true. He notes the following possibilities:

Suppose that a wife were hopelessly in love with another married man and were driven to suicide because of her moral scruples, would not her husband have every reason to reproach himself for her deed? Or, suppose that the situation were reversed? A young man, hopelessly in love with a woman who insists on remaining faithful to her husband, finds in suicide the only escape from an intolerable condition. Is not the husband bound to ask himself whether he is worth the sacrifice whether it would not have been a thousand times better for his wife to have yielded to her lover?

The latter possibility furnished Schnitzler with the theme for *Das weite Land*, a drama in which faithfulness and faithlessness in married life are treated from various angles.

Before undertaking to develop this theme in greater detail, the Viennese writer seeks to reach a temporary decision as to the dramatic or narrative form best suited for his material. The normal type of domestic tragedy would not be the best medium for shedding light upon his problem, because he is not primarily interested in the conflict of wills, morals, personalities, or ideas that may perhaps have impelled the young man to his fatal end. His center of interest is laid after the suicide. He wants to probe the effect of this incident upon the marital relationship. This suicide, because of unrequited love, can, therefore, serve only as the incentive moment in the dramatic action. It definitely sets at rest any possible doubts as to the woman's fidelity, so that the main question can be presented with perfect clarity. Schnitzler wonders whether one dialogue between husband and wife would not suffice to bring out every phase of the situation—whether, by depicting the first meeting between them immediately after the husband's return from the young man's funeral, he might not succeed in skillfully compressing within the confines of a single conversation all that ought to be said on the subject.

No sooner is this possibility weighed, however, than another becomes apparent. Since it is the husband alone who must make the necessary psychic adjustment (the wife has already reached her decision to love and be faithful at any cost; otherwise, the young man's suicide would be inexplainable), the role of the wife in any dialogue would be largely that of a listener. It is evident from Schnitzler's original concept that his purpose from the very beginning must have been to show that the woman's extreme faithfulness, instead of bringing her husband nearer to her, causes him, on the contrary, to regard her as a monster of virtue, as an instrument of death, from which he turns away in horror. To carry out Schnitzler's purpose, interest must be centered upon the husband's wrestling with his unstable emotions. The husband feels, on the one hand, that he ought to be grateful to his wife for her indubitable proof of fidelity. He feels, on the other hand, a certain aversion to her just because of her bragging Puritanism and unshakable saintliness. If our attention is to be devoted primarily to the husband, then the monologue form, such as Schnitzler masterfully employs in *Leutnant Gustl* and *Fräulein Else*, would certainly be preferable to the dialogue form. We could follow the mental processes of the husband as he returns from the funeral. One thought association leads to another, and gradually the experiences of the past and the fears of the future are unrolled from the vantage point of the present. Such a soliloquy may have either a tragic undertone, as in *Fräulein Else*, or a comic undertone, as in *Leutnant Gustl*. Schnitzler considers both possibilities. The hero may be driven insane by brooding over this matter. Or, he may give expression to his vexation in a farcical manner, as in the following outline: "God! Let her lie with my porter. If only my friend could rearise! Women—how many there are! But a friend—especially such as he! Well, what am I to do? I must go home. How beautiful everything would be, if he were still alive! I won't touch her, this murderess!" After weighing the advantages of both forms, Schnitzler finally decides to sketch a monologue which avoids the extremes of farce and of tragedy. This monologue is written on May 1, 1902, and is preserved among Schnitzler's manuscripts under the title *Frieberg-Novelle*.

Frieberg is the prototype of Friedrich Hofreiter. Since

his wife insists upon taking her marriage vows seriously, he must, by contrast, be depicted as a flirt, for whom the pursuit of women is but a pleasant pastime—as an older Anatol, to whom love is still a temporary amusement and faithfulness merely a word with which to beguile trusting ears. To such a person, the death of his friend, because of hopeless love, must seem shocking, if not inexplicable; and the behavior of his wife, ridiculous, if not inhuman. He does not understand why everyone assumes that, now, he ought to feel proud of himself. He is afraid to go home from the cemetery. He fears to face his wife in her present "super-virtuous" mood. He is sorry for his friend, whose death was so wholly unnecessary. What if his friend had been success-ful in love! No one would have suffered any loss. He, the husband, need not have learned of this affair, especially since he is a husband who betrays his wife with all sorts of women. But, he reasons on, husbands do find out. And then, moreover, his friend would have been no less dead at the present moment, for he, Frieberg, would probably have been obliged to act the part of the avenging husband and to kill his wife's lover in a duel.

In the course of the soliloquy, Frieberg thus arrives at two startling conclusions. In the first place, his friend is, alas, dead because of unrequited love. If he had not commit-ted suicide, this friend would, alas, have had to die because of requited love. In the second place, Frieberg is angry with his wife because she did not avert the suicide by yielding to her lover. On the other hand, however, he would have had to be angry with her for yielding to her lover, though this might have been necessary to avert the suicide.

If, however, the conclusions may be thus worded, then, would they not be better incorporated in a tragi-comedy than in a monologue? Might not the ideal form be a tragi-comedy in three acts? The first act would depict life in the Frieberg villa: the husband is carrying on an affair with another woman; his friend is hopelessly in love with the wife, and on this account commits suicide. The second act would begin with the wife's confession to her husband, who does not feel at all flattered by her act but is, rather, chagrined. The third act would reach a climax when the husband espies someone descending from his wife's window, and shoots him; then the wife complains that one can never please such a husband, no matter how one acts.

An outline of this kind is, indeed, to be found among Schnitzler's manuscripts. It is not, however, until the summer of 1908, six years after the *Frieberg-Novelle*, that the author begins recasting the original plot, in order to make it fit into the mould of a tragi-comedy. During these years Schnitzler has been occupied mainly with his "semi-autobiographic" novel, *Der Weg ins Freie*, which he began in 1902 but did not complete until 1907. Its figures, its tone, and its atmosphere still haunt him when he resumes his development of the Frieberg theme. In an outline of June 25, 1908, he considers Felician Wergenthin as a possible character, perhaps as the second, and more successful, lover of Mrs. Frieberg. In a sketch begun three days later, the very first scene contains comments on the Jewish question that might well form a continuation of similar discussions in the novel. Frieberg, who has now been assigned the name of Friedrich Welsberg, speaks with pride of his Jewish ancestry. He is reminded of earlier days when he was less race-conscious—when, indeed, he had made up his mind not to have any children, so that the race might die out. This opening scene, moreover, takes place at the gate of the cemetery. One of the mourners recalls having seen the deceased three days earlier in the company of Baron Wergenthin and Stanzides. Though in the final version Demeter Stanzides is the only character taken over by name from the novel, nevertheless, it is apparent that other characters of *Der Weg ins Freie* would be equally at home in the salon of Friedrich Welsberg, or Friedrich Hofreiter, as he is afterwards called. Similarly, the figures of the drama would not be out of place, if they were to drop in at the Ehrenbergs, together with Georg Wergenthin and Heinrich Bermann.

In the nine chapters of *Der Weg ins Freie*, Schnitzler sought to give a complete panorama of the Viennese society that he knew best. In the nine acts which he outlined for *Das weite Land* on June 25, 1908, he wished to present a similar section of this life, with its comic overtones and its tragic undertones. This wish accounts for the increase in the number of his characters and for the complexity of their interrelation. In the version of the drama upon which he worked from August 26 until October 18, 1908, as well as in the revised final version which occupied him from the second to the twenty-fourth of February, 1909, Schnitzler struggled to unify and to condense his material, a task in which he succeeded only to a limited extent.

Before entering upon the wealth of ideas that crowd the later drafts, it may be well to restate the original theme. Schnitzler began by questioning the general assumption that a wife should always be faithful to her husband. While neither denying nor affirming this assumption, he did succeed in casting doubt upon it—a procedure which he usually followed when analyzing so-called vital problems. He portrayed a situation in which the wife caused a young man's suicide because she would not yield to his passionate entreaties. For this act her husband reproached her. Such a husband could only reproach her if he himself set little value upon her love, or upon womanly fidelity in general. He must, therefore, be an "Anatol" type, for whom death is a horrible reality to be shunned at all costs while love is merely a form of sport. If he upbraids his wife for not having given herself to her lover under these circumstances, how will he react when his wife follows his example and advice, and does not refuse the next young man who is inflamed by her presence? He has reason to assume that he will take her infidelity lightly. But will he?

He himself, as an aging Anatol, ought to be shown in affairs with other women. One such affair might be with a young girl who is fascinated by him, the man of many adventures, even as Johanna Wegrath is fascinated by Stefan von Sala, in *Der einsame Weg;* or Leonilda, by Sylvester Thorn, in *Der Gang zum Weiher*. Another affair might be with a married woman, whose husband seems to condone her escapades, perhaps because he does not wish to break up his home and deprive his children of their mother.

We thus see how the original situation brought to Schnitzler the main characters: Friedrich Hofreiter; his wife, Genia; the young ensign, Otto Aigner; the young girl, Erna Wahl; the banker, Natter; and his wife, Adele. It also suggested to Schnitzler the relations between Friedrich and Erna, between Genia and Otto, and between Friedrich and Adele. It even suggested a striking parallel between Genia's position and that of the banker, a parallel which found expression in a scene between the two characters, written by the dramatist in July, 1908, but deleted in the final version.

In the six years that elapsed since the *Frieberg-Novelle*, a new problem had seized upon Schnitzler's imagination—a problem which was to cast its mellow shade upon most of his works for the next quarter of a century—the problem of old age. He had treated it in detail for the first time in *Der einsame Weg*, the drama centering about the artist Julian Fichtner. The fate of this aging bachelor was so bitter because he had neither home nor responsible calling, no one to whom he belonged nor anyone who belonged to him. But would his fate have been any less tragic, or would his old age have been any less lonely, if he had been the husband of a loving wife, a successful business man, a sportsman, and a social lion? In Friedrich Hofreiter, Schnitzler has visualized such a character: a man who is a manufacturer and a tennis star, who is married to a faithful wife, but who is still able to charm other women. Surely Friedrich cannot be expected to resign himself as passively to the ills and privations of old age as did Julian. Like Ibsen's Master Builder, he will fight the inroads of the younger generation. But will his utmost efforts avail him anything?

Friedrich, as the symbol of age resisting youth, gains enormously in interest and sympathy over his prototype of the *Frieberg-Novelle*, who was merely an understanding and tolerant philanderer. His erotic excursions outside of his family now appear as the convulsions of a soul struck by the first darts of advancing death. He is still in the fullness of his powers. He can still defeat the youthful Otto in tennis, but his margin from a score of nine to eight is very slender. Spurred on by the youthful Erna, he can still climb the Aigner Tower in the Tyrolese Dolomites. But he well knows that this must be his last attempt to reach the peak, if he wishes to avoid the fate of Ibsen's Master Solness. Can he, under these circumstances, regard with tolerant indifference the love relation between Otto and his wife, as he theoretically assumed he could when he reproached her for not yielding to Otto's predecessor? Is he not likely to see in the situation, first and foremost, youth's triumph over age?

By interlocking this problem of youth versus age with the original problem of faithfulness in married life, it was almost inevitable that the former should exercise the stronger dramatic appeal, and that it should ultimately dominate the action. In the version of 1908, among the first words uttered by Friedrich are words of sorrow that he has been expelled from the ranks of youth. "Do you really believe," he asks, "that a man of forty-two and one of twenty-four can be friends? I tell you, it's a gulf that can never be bridged. A king and an anarchist may be friends, if they are both young. Likewise, a coquette and a respectable woman, when they are both young, and especially when they are both old. An anti-Semitic student and a Zionist—yes. But, one who puts out to sea and one who is entering the harbor—never." "If one knew at twenty how fortunate one is to be twenty," Friedrich adds, "then one would get a stroke because of sheer bliss."

In young Otto Aigner, Friedrich faces impetuous youth, that calls upon him to yield to his successors and to retire from the field of battling passions and soaring ambitions. In the duel between the two, Friedrich shoots to kill, not so much because he wishes to avenge his family honor as because he wishes to stamp out insolent youth, that demands his abdication. And yet, abdicate he must! Though the twenty-year-old Erna is still willing to link her fate to his, he has learned his lesson and refuses her offer. Though she tells him that she is convinced that they belong to each other, he replies on the basis of his newly gained insight: "You are mistaken. You are still under the influence of the result of this duel. Probably it impresses you that I . . . but you're under an illusion. Everything is illusion. Pretty soon I'll break down. It's all over between us, Erna. You are twenty, you do *not* belong to me." "You are younger than all others," Erna exclaims. "Please! I know what youth is," answers Friedrich. "Less than an hour ago, I saw it sparkle and laugh in insolent, cold eyes. I know what youth is. And I can't shoot every . . ."

The center of dramatic interest has thus gradually shifted to the new theme; namely, the conflict of generations: age giving way to youth. But this theme is best exemplified in the tragic relations between parents and children. A dramatist who seeks to present the conflict of generations in its most pathetic and universal aspect ought not to avoid this tragedy within the family. Nor does Schnitzler sidetrack this possibility. Since, however, in *Der einsame Weg*, he had dissected the relations between fathers and children, he now preferred to submit to dramatic analysis the relations between mothers and children. He, therefore, assigned to Genia Hofreiter a son, Percy; to Adele Natter, a son and a daughter; to Erna Wahl, a mother; and to Otto Aigner, a mother, Mrs. Meinhold-Aigner. Having projected these women into the tragi-comedy, Schnitzler was faced with the task of differentiating them as human beings and as mothers. He does this most skillfully in a very few words, chiefly in words exchanged between Genia and the three other women.

Mrs. Wahl is the least interesting of the group, perhaps because one cannot imagine her venturing beyond the bounds of social decorum. As the mother of the courageous, outspoken, and unconventional Erna, she is excessively timid, uncertain of her opinions, and extremely conventional. She always qualifies her every assertion with an "if" and a "but," in order not to offend. She is continually shocked by Erna's frankness, and feels it her duty to explain and to apologize for her. Because she tries to exercise guardianship over her daughter's morals, the dramatist, with sardonic glee, lets Friedrich lead Erna astray, almost under her very eyes, while she, suspecting nothing, upbraids him for having caused her anxiety by undertaking a dangerous mountain tour with her daughter.

Adele Natter, less conventional than Mrs. Wahl, has had an affair with Friedrich; but, now that her two children are growing up, she realizes that the period of her youthful follies ought to come to an end. She may still accept the attentions of Stanzides, but before long she will return to her family responsibilities. She is on the road to becoming a faithful wife and a devoted mother. Her husband has been waiting for this moment. Even as Genia loves Friedrich, in spite of his infidelity so, too, Mr. Natter loves his wife, though aware of her "extra-marital" escapades. Now he may confidently expect a renaissance of their former affectionate relations.

Genia is the born mother. It is to her that Dr. Mauer, the *raisonneur* of the drama, refers when he remarks that women who are born to be mothers often have the gift of being such even toward their husbands. She fears for Friedrich as though he were her child. She trembles lest Natter avenge himself for the dishonor to his family, and she forgets her own grievances in her concern for her husband. She goes so far as to continue to remain on friendly terms with Adele, and to invite Adele's children to her home. She takes for granted her own faithfulness.

When Friedrich rebukes her for unwittingly causing a young man's death, she tries to please him by accepting the overtures of young Otto Aigner, in order to prevent a possible second suicide. She is, however, not fashioned for illicit relations. No sooner has she given herself to Otto than she is overwhelmed by the hideousness of her deed. She has broken the simple tenets of her faith; she has lost her moral hold; and she feels herself gliding toward the unknown. "Why do you regard me as better than I am?" she asks her lover. "I am not better than others. Can't you see it? I lie. I am hypocritical. I carry on a comedy before others—before Mr. Natter and before Mrs. Wahl, before your mother as well as before my chambermaid. I play the role of the respectable woman; and at night I leave my window open for my lover. I write my son that he may stay longer with his friends. I write this to my dear son in order that he shouldn't interrupt my adventure; and I write my husband that Percy insists on staying in Richmond, so that he, too, might stay away longer. And today, when he comes back and shakes hands with you, I'll stand near by, and smile, and probably rejoice at my skillfulness. Do you find all this very beautiful? Do you think that I am a woman to be trusted? Believe me, Otto, I'm just like the others." Genia's outburst is a symptom of moral nostalgia. She will be cured of her disgust with herself after her Percy arrives, when she can give vent to her motherly instincts. She nourishes the hope of finding, in perfect understanding and communion with her son, a compensation for her unhappy marriage.

Mrs. Meinhold-Aigner has no such illusions. She has frankly capitulated to the younger generation, and she does not feel obliged to maintain even a semblance of authority over her Otto. She reminds Genia that sons, also, grow up to be men. "There is one illusion from which we can never free ourselves too soon, Genia; namely, that we can hold on forever to our children. Especially sons! They have *us*, but we don't have them. I think that one is even more painfully conscious of this fact, if one always lives under the same roof with them. As long as they are small, they sell us for a toy; and afterwards—afterwards, for still less." In accordance with this view, Mrs. Meinhold wisely refrains from interfering with her son, even though she perceives that he is entering on a dangerous path. She is the understanding mother. She must suffer and tremble in silence, as she watches her offspring venture out on perilous trails. She has experienced so much pain herself that she knows the futility of all interference with the workings of fate. Human beings live as they must. Twenty years ago she might still, perhaps, have flared up when she discovered her husband's infidelity. Though she has been separated from him all these years, she has not forgotten his deception. However, now that she has accepted a tolerant, resigned attitude, it seems absurd to condemn her husband, or even to feel angry with him.

Dr. Aigner himself appears in the play as a hotel director of a Tyrolese mountain resort, at which several of the dramatic characters meet. If Friedrich Hofreiter may be regarded as the successor of Julian Fichtner, then Dr. Aigner may be said to take the place of Stefan von Sala. The conversation between the two aging egoists, in *Das weite Land*, seems like a continuation of those engaged in by their prototypes, in *Der einsame Weg*. Dr. Aigner confesses that he loves his wife, and yet he has repeatedly betrayed her. He feels it his duty to tell her about his other affairs, in order not to appear cowardly in her eyes, and also, perhaps, because it is most convenient not to be burdened with secrets. From that moment, however, her faith in him is gone, and family life based on mutual confidence becomes absolutely impossible. When Friedrich asks him why he has betrayed the woman he loves, Aigner pleads, as his only excuse, the complexity of the human soul. "There is room for so much in us at the same time! Love and treachery faith and faithlessness . . . adoration of one person and longing for another, or for several others. We try to bring order into ourselves as best as we can; but this order is, after all, something artificial . . . Our natural state is chaos. Yes, my good Hofreiter, the soul is a vast panorama."

The complexity of existence forms the keynote of the drama and the ultimate explanation for the paradoxical behavior of its characters. Human acts and human emotions are the result of many shifting and interlocked causes that may reach back even beyond the birth of consciousness. Hence, none are guilty. All live as they must. All act as they are impelled. Let us, therefore, not judge, Schnitzler would emphasize; and, above all, let us hesitate to condemn. For, the soul *is* a vast panorama.

CHAPTER IX

THE PHYSICIANS' DRAMA

Schnitzler, who devoted his literary talent to an analysis of the psychic and social ills of the people about him, was often tempted to treat of the problems of the medical profession, which was originally his own, and to portray the various types of doctors among whom he had grown up. Not only were his father and his brother outstanding physicians at the Austrian capital, but, as we have seen, he himself had devoted the greater part of his youth to the study of medicine. From 1879 to 1885 he was matriculated at the University of Vienna; and, after obtaining his medical degree in the latter year, he remained for three years as an intern and assistant at a clinic, and then devoted additional years to specializing in psychiatry. He attended medical conventions at Berlin and London, contributed articles to Viennese medical journals, and became practically an authority on hypnotism and suggestion.

Schnitzler's literary work betrays the influence of his professional training. In *Anatol* and in *Paracelsus*, he skillfully introduced hypnotic phenomena into the dramatic action. In *Sterben*, he tried to explain the gradual dissolution of the hero's moral and psychic personality by an exact narration of the latter's physical decay. In several dramas the physician acts as the ideal *raisonneur*, who knows the clinical history of the contending characters and who can, therefore, properly advise and heal. Such calm and wise physicians are Dr. Reumann, in *Der einsame Weg;* Dr.

Schindler, in *Der Ruf des Lebens;* and Dr. Mauer, in *Das weite Land.*

As early as 1899, Schnitzler conceived the idea of centering a play about some problem of the physician's calling—a problem that would enable him to give as complete as possible a cross section of the medical world. At first he considered treating of the complications that might arise from a conflict between the scientific and the religious attitudes towards the sick. Such complications would follow if a physician, who regarded it as his duty to gladden the last hours of a dying patient, were to prevent a priest from administering the last rites to this person. The physician might act thus in the following situation: if the patient imagined himself on the road to recovery, and the doctor feared that the entrance of the priest would wrest from the dying person his last, pleasant dreams and would subject him to unnecessary, horrible disillusionment.

The first draft, of the year 1899, preserved among Schnitzler's manuscripts, reads as follows: "A physician expels a priest who wishes to administer the last sacrament to a dying person, because this dying person imagines himself healthy and does not suspect that he is at death's door."

This simple situation might be treated either in the form of a tale or a drama. If the narrative form is selected, then the plot might be presented from the viewpoint of the physician, who feels that, when he can no longer cure, he can, at least, comfort; and that he ought, if necessary, to construct a rainbow bridge of lies over which he may enable the patient to pass on with the minimum of fear and suffering to the Beyond. The situation might also be presented from the viewpoint of the priest, who holds that the salvation of the soul is so very important that it outweighs the temporary pain caused by the patient's realization that all hope is gone. Since Schnitzler does not share the theological viewpoint, he is all the more tempted to emphasize the argument in its favor, in order to convince us of its fundamental cruelty through the very words of its staunchest defender.

Schnitzler employs this technique repeatedly in his tales of this period. In *Leutnant Gustl* (1900), he wants to expose the ridiculousness of the code of honor which prescribes the conduct of officers. He does this by speaking through the voice of Gustl, its sturdiest defender. In *Andreas Thamayers letzter Brief* (1900), he lets the hero present all available proof that he, Andreas, and no one else, is the father of his wife's colored child. From this proof the reader deduces the opposite conclusion—namely, that Andreas cannot possibly be the father; and though this hero is willing to make the supreme sacrifice for his belief, the reader remains unconvinced. The second draft of the physician's theme, therefore, ends with the note: "*Vom Priester aus gesehen.*"

According to this second draft, the patient is a girl who does not suspect that her death is imminent. She comes from a religious family. The Jewish physician, because of unpleasant experiences in similar cases, wishes her to receive the last rites. Her betrothed, who is present, refuses to admit the priest. As the patient enters from her sick chamber, she catches sight of the priest. Up to this moment she has remained persuaded that she is on the road to recovery. Now the fear of death takes possession of her.

In this second draft, there are several important changes and additions to be noted. The adversary of the priest is no longer the physician; instead, he is the patient's betrothed.

The conflict is, therefore, very clearly between the religious duty of the priest, who wants to save a sinner's soul from perdition, and the humane duty of the layman, who wants to spare his beloved needless suffering. The physician might ordinarily be expected to espouse the cause of the fiancée. To eliminate this possibility and to provide a neutral observer for the conflict, Schnitzler makes the physician Jewish. Such a doctor knows from past experience that his interference is likely to be misinterpreted. By remaining silently neutral, the physician strengthens the priest's position, since the latter can point out that the doctor, though a Jew, does not question the propriety of ministering to a dying soul. This argument is especially valuable if the material is presented solely from the viewpoint of the priest. Moreover, should Schnitzler convert his material into dramatic form, then he would have in his physician the ideal observer, who is excellently qualified to comment on the action—a *raisonneur* comparable to Dr. Reumann, in *Der einsame Weg*, or Dr. Mauer, in *Das weite Land*. At this stage, Schnitzler has, as yet, no intention of complicating his problem by an elaborate discussion of the relations between Jews and their neighbors—a theme most prominent in the final version.

The narrative or drama of the physician's calling had reached this point of development, when, at the turn of the century, Schnitzler began to work on *Der einsame Weg*. As we have seen in a preceding chapter, an intermediate, unpublished version of this play deals with the question as to whether a physician has a right to administer poison to a person incurably ill, in order to ease the latter's suffering. The patient is Mrs. Pflugfelder; and the opposing viewpoints are held by her husband and by her son, both of them physicians. Professor Bernhardi is the specialist whose aid is requested by the Pflugfelder family. Since Schnitzler found himself with two possible dramas of the physician's calling on his hands at the same time, he faced the dilemma of choosing between them. On the one hand, he could treat of the conflict between the doctor's obligation to ease human pain and his obligation to prolong life to the last possible moment. On the other hand, he might dramatize the conflict between the humane duty of preventing unnecessary suffering and the religious duty of ministering to the soul of the dying.

Since the former theme could be more easily combined with the material centering about the lonely bachelor, Julian Fichtner, and his doomed friend, Stefan von Sala, Schnitzler composed, during 1902 and the first few months of 1903, a drama in five acts, which he entitled *Der einsame Weg* and which included medical discussions by the Pflugfelders and Professor Bernhardi. Young Pflugfelder supplies his hopelessly sick mother with poison, in order to relieve her intense pain; but before long he is made to realize the wrongness of his act. This theme, at first intended merely as a minor episode to motivate Julian Fichtner's behavior in laying claim to his estranged son after the death of the mother, assumed such importance during the writing of the various acts that it dominated the entire atmosphere and dramatic action. If Schnitzler, therefore, wished to restore the emphasis originally placed on the problem of the lonely bachelor and that of the son between two fathers, he was forced to cut out the medical material, and to reserve it for a play distinct from *Der einsame Weg*. He did this in the spring of 1903. The first outline of the new play bore the title *Verurteilte* and projected as likely characters Professor

Bernhardi; Stefan von Sala; and the Pflugfelder family, consisting of Dr. Pflugfelder, his wife, his son Hans, and his daughter Johanna. At about the same time, however, Schnitzler, who was busy recasting *Der einsame Weg*, found that he could not dispense with Sala as the companion of Julian. Sala had, therefore, to be removed from the planned *Verurteilte*, and with him went his beloved Johanna. Their loss was compensated for by assigning to Professor Bernhardi a son, Josef, and to Dr. Pflugfelder a daughter, Anna. The two families could then be linked together by love and marriage, as well as by common professional interests.

A detailed outline, preserved among the dramatist's drafts, gives us an insight into the physician's play, as envisaged by Schnitzler in May, 1903. Three acts are planned. The first act is to take place at the home of Bernhardi just before he leaves on a vacation. We are introduced to his mediocre wife, who can offer him much kindness but only little understanding. We make the acquaintance of his son, who is a fairly decent person, but who has hardly any talent. Bernhardi senses the hollowness of his own life. He is disgusted with conditions, and even thinks of resigning from the medical faculty. Perhaps there are charges of unprofessional conduct lodged against him. A typical charge might be that he disavowed, or expelled, a colleague for prophesying to a patient an early death. In this new guise we recognize an echo of the original plan of 1899, when the physician expelled the priest so that the patient might remain ignorant of the approaching end. The Professor of Anatomy, who is, also, Dean of the Medical School, tells Bernhardi of two unusual cases at the latter's clinic. A chemical analysis has showed that in both cases death resulted, not from the disease certified by Bernhardi, but

rather from an excessive dose of morphium. Bernhardi
promises to look into the matter. The Pflugfelders arrive.
Hans Pflugfelder is Bernhardi's clinical assistant. Fearing
that Mrs. Pflugfelder is suffering from an incurable disease,
Hans asks Bernhardi to give her a thorough examination.
This examination confirms the original diagnosis made by
her son. She cannot be saved. "How horrible! If only one
could kill!" exclaims Hans. Bernhardi's suspicions are
aroused. He counsels lying to patients.

The second act takes place at the Pflugfelder home.
Anna Pflugfelder and young Bernhardi are to be engaged.
In a conversation between Hans and his mother, we learn
of the last service that she expects of him. Just because he
loves her so much, he cannot let her suffer needlessly, when
all hope of recovery is gone.

The third act takes place after the sudden death of Mrs.
Pflugfelder. The Professor of Anatomy informs Bernhardi
that her death was caused by poisoning. Hans assumes full
responsibility for shortening his mother's life. He undertakes
to atone for his crime by offering his services as a physician
on a dangerous expedition to India. His father approves this
form of atonement.

This brief summary of the main medical problem leaves
unmentioned the minor characters and secondary themes
with which the outline abounds. A new figure, occurring
in this and succeeding drafts, is Dr. Binz, afterwards
renamed Dr. Feuerstein. This physician has studied with
Hans, but, because of poverty, he has had to enter practice
immediately after graduation. As a result, he needlessly
brings about the death of a woman who should have been
saved. He, therefore, loses his medical license. In order to
gain reinstatement in the medical profession, he asks

Bernhardi to intercede for him. In their conversations, as well as in those between Bernhardi and the Pflugfelders, the dramatist has an opportunity to interpolate his views on the medical profession.

Though he had worked out in detail the outline for the drama, Schnitzler did not proceed any further with the physician's play until six years later. Meanwhile he completed *Der einsame Weg*. The roles originally assigned in this play to Professor Bernhardi and the Pflugfelders were turned over to Dr. Reumann and the Wegrath family. Soon thereafter Schnitzler began *Der Ruf des Lebens*, the drama in which Marie Moser hastens the death of her bed-ridden father, partly in order to spare him additional years of torture, and partly also in order to be free to answer the lure of love. The physician of this play, Dr. Schindler, has the characteristics of Professor Bernhardi and is probably based upon the same model. While Dr. Schindler may not approve of Marie's act, he does not condemn her as a criminal; instead, he comforts her during her distressed state of mind and shows her a way of atoning. He suggests to her that she enter the service as a nurse near the battlefront—a form of atonement similar to the one that Hans Pflugfelder imposed upon himself, after having hastened his mother's end.

In *Der Weg ins Freie*, the novel to which Schnitzler devoted his best efforts from 1902 to 1907, Heinrich Bermann maintains that at some future time it will be regarded as a crime to prolong the life of a person who is doomed to a painful and long, drawn-out end. Young Dr. Berthold Stauber believes that a comprehensive plan for social hygiene ought to aim at dispensing with all harmful and useless members of society.

In sketching a physician's play after the appearance of

Der einsame Weg, Der Ruf des Lebens, and *Der Weg ins Freie*, Schnitzler could not, therefore, any longer make use of the main theme he had outlined in May, 1903. Fragmentary notes bear witness to his continued search for a new central theme that would let him illumine problems of the medical calling. For a moment he considered constructing a physician's drama about a possible conflict between so-called professional conduct and real humane behavior. For example, after one physician has pronounced a case hopeless and the patient despairs of recovery, another physician disavows the former's diagnosis and thereby restores the patient's hope and will to live. The first physician complains that his successor has not acted the part of an ethical colleague in this matter.

Another possible theme noted by Schnitzler retains Professor Bernhardi as the leading character. He has rounded a large medical institute, but, being a Jew, he is opposed by ambitious anti-Semites. His struggles against this obnoxious clique would supply fruitful material for a colorful plot. This theme attracted Schnitzler's imagination, because in developing it he could make use of certain experiences that members of his own immediate circle must have gone through in hospitals and clinics. Furthermore, that he was at this time troubled more and more by the Jewish question is evident from the discussions which he interpolated in *Der Weg ins Freie*.

In seeking for a basis of conflict between Professor Bernhardi and his anti-Semitic opponents, Schnitzler reverted to his draft of 1899. Bernhardi's refusal to admit the priest to the room of the dying patient supplies his adversaries with an excellent opportunity for unjustified anti-Jewish incitements. Schnitzler himself had not been spared misunderstandings and unjustified attacks after the publication of *Der Weg ins Freie*. He saw in the drama about Professor Bernhardi an occasion to reply to his detractors and to show how a minor incident could be so misconstrued by prejudiced parties that it might assume the proportions of a major scandal which would bring down upon its central figure undeserved calumny and equally undeserved martyrdom.

On October 23, 1909, Schnitzler outlined the new plot of *Professor Bernhardi* in the form of a five-act drama. On November 4, he made an attempt to condense the material into three acts. Then he began the actual writing of the individual scenes. On March 25, 1911, he noted the necessity for recasting the play into five acts. In 1912, the completed drama made its appearance, arousing, as its author probably anticipated, official condemnation and popular approval.

The final published version is unique in that it has no female characters outside of a nurse, and in that it contains hardly any references to love or sex. Our study of the origin of the drama has supplied us with the explanation. We have seen how these characters and references were absorbed by other works to which Schnitzler was simultaneously devoting his creative talents.

In a hospital ward, a young girl is dying of blood-poisoning. In her last hours of life, she enters a psychic state, well known to physicians, in which she loses all sensation of pain and imagines herself recovering. Just as Professor Bernhardi, the director of the hospital, leaves her, he meets at the entrance to the ward a priest who has been called by the Catholic nurse and who has come to administer the last sacrament to the dying girl. Bernhardi feels that it is his duty as a physician not to upset the unsuspecting patient, who believes herself improving. In a calm tone he asks the priest not to enter the sick chamber. When the latter insists, Bernhardi, thinking only of his duty towards his patient, forbids him to pass. The dispute waxes intense. Meanwhile the zealous nurse has informed the girl of the arrival of the priest, so that, contrary to the doctor's intentions, death does not descend upon the patient while she is in the midst of pleasant dreams.

Bernhardi's attitude is misrepresented by his adversaries and only half-heartedly upheld by his friends. The trustees, who support the Medical Institute financially and morally, threaten to resign. The clerical group of deputies prepares to bring the matter to the attention of the government. Bernhardi does not wish to endanger the Institute, which he himself has rounded, nor to become the center of political machinations. He is, therefore, ready to end the affair by offering a dignified explanation of his action. The unscrupulous behavior of his adversaries, however, induces him to take an energetic stand. The situation is complicated by the fact that Bernhardi is Jewish, a not unmitigated blessing in Vienna at the turn of the century. The unexpected visit of Dr. Flint, the new Minister of Education, enables Bernhardi to present his side of the case. Twenty-five years before, the two were clinical assistants at the same hospital. Though Flint, like many other professors on the medical faculty, opposed Bernhardi's Institute when it was being established, nevertheless, he now assures the director that in the ensuing struggle Bernhardi can count on his support.

The climax of the agitation is reached at a meeting of the professors at the Institute. With masterful strokes, various types of physicians are portrayed: the pure scientist;

the unprincipled politician; the fawning sycophant; the renegade Jew, who hates his former coreligionists; and the hot-headed Jew, who suspects foes everywhere. Among these physicians, Bernhardi shines forth as a dispassionate, unsentimental, kind-hearted human being. He refuses to be embroiled in politics. He seeks to avoid the limelight. When the trustees resign and the Minister, for personal and party reasons, promises to start an investigation of the exaggerated incident, Bernhardi voluntarily retires from his directorship in order not to increase factional strife among his colleagues.

As a result of the investigation and trial, he is found guilty of forcibly hindering a priest in the exercise of his sacred duty, and is condemned to two-months' imprisonment. His lawyer suggests appealing the case. Professor Pflugfelder, Bernhardi's chief supporter, wants to call mass meetings to arouse public opinion. The society of freethinkers volunteers its help. The reporter of a liberal paper brings an offer from the editor to let Bernhardi renew the battle in the press, and especially to let him attack the Minister of Education. Bernhardi refuses all intercession. He insists again and again that he is not interested in politics. He wants to get through with his sentence as soon as possible, so that he can return to his practice.

Bernhardi's stand is emphasized by the author throughout the fourth and fifth acts of the drama. Even after public opinion has veered in favor of the unjustly imprisoned physician, and even when, upon the expiration of his sentence, he can successfully effect a revision of the judicial error, he still refuses to lift a finger in his own behalf. He refuses to be made the plaything of politicians. He is first and foremost a scientist. His profession is to cure people.

Schnitzler holds this calling to be more productive of human happiness than the calling of the politician. In a final scene between Bernhardi and the Minister of Education, whom the physician visits in order to regain his forfeited medical license, Schnitzler arranges a juxtaposition of the two types: the scientist who fearlessly pursues the path of his honest convictions, and the man of public affairs who must constantly alter his views to conform with changing political constellations.

Bernhardi's stand resembles that of old Dr. Stauber, in *Der Weg ins Freie*. When the latter's son Berthold, outraged at unfair anti-Semitic attacks, gives up his political career in order to resume his study of bacteriology, the father heartily endorses the young man's decision. When Berthold, however, a year later accepts a nomination to the Austrian Parliament and thereby again turns his back upon medicine, his father wisely points out the futility of engaging in such activity. One cannot serve two masters. If the choice lies between science and politics, the older physician insists that it is absurd to give up the positive task of healing for the doubtful privilege of haranguing people whose minds are mostly made up in advance, or of combatting opponents who generally do not themselves believe the tenets they pretend to defend. Especially is it absurd for a Jew to interfere in his country's political squabbles. In the field of science even a Jew may hope to earn his laurels and to contribute to human welfare. In the field of politics, however, he will be made to feel at every turn that he is an unwelcome stranger, though his ancestors may have sojourned in the land close to two thousand years.

In *Professor Bernhardi*, Schnitzler gives profound utterance to his views on the place of the Jew in modern life.

The Jewish question troubled him throughout many years. It subjected him to several unpleasant, and even dangerous, experiences. He was, no less than his hero, Bernhardi, the target for anti-Semitic attacks. Once, while on a visit to Prague, he barely escaped physical injury at the hands of "Jew-baiting" youths. To this day his name is anathema to certain sections of the central European population. Nevertheless, in his literary treatment of the Jewish question, he managed to retain his wonted philosophic calm. He pleaded the cause of no single party. He advocated no royal road to salvation. He merely brought to bear upon a very complex question the light of a kind and critical temperament. His views on the Jew in contemporary life, expressed in *Der Weg ins Freie*, in *Professor Bernhardi*, and in *Der Gang zum Weiher*, are pregnant with wisdom and are well worth careful study.

CHAPTER X

A CONFESSION OF FAITH

IN grappling with the Jewish problem, Schnitzler does not minimize its difficulty. He does not mask its ugliness. He makes no predictions as to its future trend. He merely lays bare a moral and social condition that brings suffering and bewilderment to millions of people. The Jewish problem has its origin, he believes, in the existence of the Jews as a minority in each nation. He holds that any human group which lives in the midst of a numerically larger group, and which retains its own peculiarities, must inevitably arouse in the majority a consciousness of difference. This consciousness usually gives birth to dislike, resentment, contempt, and hate. It should not, but it does. It may manifest itself in mild forms of injustice and slander, or in the more brutal forms of murder and pogroms. This anthropological law will apply to all peoples irrespective of their specific characteristics. Thus, if Aryans should happen to be in a minority in any country, anti-Aryanism would immediately develop. Attention would be focused upon all the faults of the Aryans from the dawn of history up to the present time. Examples of cruelty, cowardice, cunning, avarice, and baseness would be collected from all periods to justify the dislike for Aryans and to refute any Aryan champion who might complain that his people deserved better treatment at the hands of the majority. Similarly, anti-Semitism is the natural outcome of the historic position in which the Jews, as a minority group, find themselves in every land; and no amount of Jewish or Christian sentimentality will eradicate this feeling. Perhaps in a thousand years the whole Jewish question will have ceased to exist; but in our generation, in our century, and as long as the sense of difference is deep-rooted in Jews and in their neighbors, no solution need be expected—at least, no general solution that will be applicable to all Jewish people. It will rather be up to each individual to adjust himself as best he may. Schnitzler discusses possible types of adjustments, and subjects to close scrutiny the two most important tendencies in contemporary Jewish life; namely, Zionism and Assimilation.

Zionism of today owes its inspiration and driving force to Theodor Herzl, a friend and admirer of Schnitzler. There is no doubt that Herzl, the fiery crusader, must have made strenuous efforts to convert the successful dramatist to the cause of Palestine. In the figure of Leo Golowsky, in *Der Weg ins Freie*, Schnitzler pays stirring tribute to Herzl and the philosophy of Zionism. The dramatist himself remains a heretic, but a heretic with considerable sympathy for those who have found a refuge in the new gospel. He agrees that, in spite of all so-called political equality, Jews are everywhere regarded as citizens of the second rank; and he can appreciate the feelings of those who are tired of being perpetual objects of well-meaning tolerance, and who would rather look upon themselves as strangers sojourning in a foreign land—strangers with a real home in some country that takes a genuine interest in their welfare. He can also justify Zionism as a philanthropic venture that offers a secure resting place for millions of his coreligionists who suffer from physical or spiritual persecution, and who would gladly exchange their Ghetto quarters for some fruitful land in which they would form a majority and in which they would be governed by their own kin. He does not, however, accept the fundamental assumption of political Zionism that this land must be Palestine. He does not believe that Jews everywhere are animated by a longing for a land of which they know little more than that their ancestors, according to tradition, lived there in some remote past. He feels that the enthusiasm for Palestine has been artificially created, and is directly traceable to the spread of anti-Semitism in Europe. Not even Herzl, the father of political Zionism, ever thought of Palestine as his fatherland, until the Dreyfus affair, in Paris, made him aware of the strong undercurrent of anti-Jewish sentiment in most European countries. If an American, whose ancestors emigrated from England, or France, or Germany a century ago, never regards these mother countries as his home, why should one expect a Jew, whose ancestors left Palestine two thousand years ago, still to cherish within his blood longings for this remote land? Palestine is not, according to Schnitzler, the home of all the Jews. For the concept of home denotes not the abode of one's ancestors, nor even the place of one's own birth; but rather it is the center of a person's activity, the circle in which he grew up, the culture to which he owes his development and in which he is most comfortable. The Viennese physician and author feels most strongly that Vienna is his home, and he loves this home more deeply than the loud-mouthed patriots who would exile him from this city if they had the power to do so. "Though all who dwell in this land from time immemorial were to shout in my face the epithet 'stranger,' and though they were even to erect the stake for me, neither their threats nor their hate could ever destroy this feeling. You, Earth, know that I have grown out of you;

and you, Heaven, know that it is *my* home on which you
are throwing your brilliant light. It is not as an outcast that
I breathe between you. "

German, and not Hebrew, is the language of his literary
masterpieces—the language he thrills to. The psyche of
central Europe is more intelligible to him than the psyche
of the Orient. He sees no justification for Zionism in the
reputed longing of the Jews for the Holy Land. He finds it
natural for Jews to be enraged at injustices committed
against them. or their kin because of racial origin, and for
them to experience in such moments a desire to go off and
settle elsewhere. He depicts in Salomon Ehrenberg, in *Der
Weg ins Freie*, a Jew whose anger and chagrin lead him to
Palestine, but who returns in a chastened mood ready to
continue the struggle against his foes in Vienna itself, the
city which is, after all, home to him. Schnitzler maintains
that it is as incorrect to speak of the Jews as homeless as
it would be to speak of those people as sleepless who are
not allowed to fall asleep, whose pillows are snatched from
under their heads, whose quilts are pulled away from them,
whose toes are tickled, and whose noses are constantly
twitted. The Jews have their homes in every country. What
they lack are fellow-citizens.

Heinrich Bermann, who, in *Der Weg ins Freie*, often
voices Schnitzler's sincerest beliefs, gives vent to his
embitterment at this state of affairs. He asks the Catholic
Baron Georg von Wergenthin: "Do you think that there is
in this world a single Christian—even assuming that he is
the noblest, fairest, and most trustworthy of men—a single
Christian who, in some moment of disappointment and anger
at his best friend, sweetheart, or wife, would not throw up
their Jewishness to them, if they happened to be Jews, or

of Jewish descent? He may not do it in so many words, but certainly he will think it in his heart of hearts. As a proof, pick up the letters of any famous person who is, in every other respect, intelligent and admirable. Read carefully the passages containing hostile and ironic comments about his contemporaries. In ninety-nine cases out of a hundred these comments concern individuals whose race and religion are not taken into account. In the hundredth case, where the attacked human being has the misfortune to be a Jew, the author certainly does not fail to mention this fact." Against the Baron's criticism that Heinrich must be suffering from "persecution-mania," the latter counters with the assertion that Jews are more likely to suffer from a "security-mania"—that they are more likely to regard themselves as safe in the house of friends, simply because they are for a time left in peace. What the Baron regards as "persecution-mania" is really nothing more than an acute awareness of the true, unstable condition in which the Jews find themselves. Every Jew, though he may have little in common with his coreligionists, feels that, somehow, in the eyes of others he is held responsible for every fault and every error committed by a fellow-Jew. Hence, his extreme sensitiveness towards any tactlessness, or any wrong-doing, of which a member of his race may be guilty. From childhood he learns through contact with his neighbors that Jewish traits are either especially funny or very disagreeable. If he, then, sees a Jew misbehaving, he is overcome by a feeling of shame similar to that which a brother would experience if his sister were to undress before him. Jews are, therefore, their own severest critics; they are the least tolerant of all people with their own race.

In *Der Weg ins Freie*, Schnitzler lets Leo Golowsky,

the Zionist, and Heinrich Bermann, the tortured skeptic, air their contradictory views on the Jewish question before the sympathetic Georg von Wergenthin. Georg, who tries to be objective, finds himself agreeing at one moment with Leo, who is too proud to impose himself upon fellow-citizens who will not accept him as their equal and who, therefore, wants to go off with his racial brothers to a land of their own. The following moment, however, Georg feels himself more nearly in accord with Heinrich, who speaks of Zionism as a fantastic and short-sighted policy, and who sees no particular gain in gathering from all ends of the world and in sending off to a strange land the members of a race, most of whom are participating to the best of their ability in the cultures of their various countries, and almost all of whom have no particular homesickness for any other abode. For the first time, Georg begins to suspect the difficult position in which the best Jews find themselves, those Jews who, on the one hand, do not want to impose themselves where they are not welcome, and who, on the other hand, are embittered by the demand that they become assimilated by the insolent majority. "For the first time, the word 'Jew,' which he had himself so often uttered thoughtlessly and even scornfully, appeared to him from a new and gloomy angle. An insight was granted him into this people's mysterious lot—an insight which affected all who sprang from its ranks: those who sought to escape from their origin as from a disgrace, pain, or fairy tale that did not concern them, as well as those others who stubbornly harped upon their origin as upon a fate, an honor, or an unalterable historic fact."

The hopelessness of all immediate solutions of this complicated problem is brought home to Georg even further when, in answer to his supposition that gradual assimilation might be the best remedy, he is disillusioned by Heinrich's painful remarks: "Assimilation . . . a word . . . yes, it will come, some day . . . in the far, far distant future. It will not come in the way some wish and others fear. It will not be exactly assimilation . . . but, perhaps, something essentially similar. Do you know what the final conclusion will probably prove? That we, we Jews I mean, were, in a sense, a ferment of humanity—yes, that will, perhaps, be realized in a thousand or two thousand years."

Until then the solution is hopeless. Schnitzler expresses this pessimistic view not merely in *Der Weg ins Freie* but also, years afterwards, in *Professor Bernhardi*. In the latter play, the Catholic priest and the Jewish physician both agree that they are separated by a gulf that cannot be wholly bridged, and that all efforts at eradicating their differences must fail. There is no reason, however, why an understanding of these differences should not take the place of mutual distrust. Understanding will efface bitterness. Understanding will prevent persecution and injustice. Understanding will further tolerance, and make life easier for all concerned.

To Schnitzler it seems very absurd for people to wrangle over questions of faith and to abuse each other because of their beliefs, or even lack of belief. What is faith, or belief? he once asked. When we say we believe, are we not merely asserting that a certain explanation appeals to us as the most plausible one for a certain phenomenon? When we say we believe in God, do we not merely state that we do not accept finite explanations as the most plausible ones for certain phenomena? In this sense, the difference between human beings is really very slight, for even so-called atheists merely substitute an equivalent concept for that which others call God—a different name, another guess. Disputes between religious creeds are waged over the acceptance or rejection of this or that mythology. These disputes could be avoided if Christianity, Judaism, and other creeds of today were studied more often in the same scientific spirit as are the creeds of ancient Assyria, Greece, or Rome; or if the facts, theories, and assumptions of religion were regarded in the same light as are those of music, biology, or astronomy. Why should the person who ridicules Darwin, Goethe, Beethoven, or Michelangelo be tolerated as a respectable member of society; and the one who mocks at Christ, or St. Francis of Assisi be looked at askance? Surely, that mysterious divine element, whatever it may turn out to be, manifested itself in Goethe and Copernicus no less than in Christ and his apostles. But no artistic or scientific genius is ever worshiped in the manner in which saints are.

Were the differences between Jews and their neighbors purely religious, reconciliation might, in that case, not be so hopeless; for there are millions of people today in whose lives organized religion plays no important role. These differences lie much deeper, however, and cannot be easily grasped in words. Georg Wergenthin, who associates much with Jews, feels that, in spite of all sympathy toward them, he will never attain the same unembarrassing intimacy with them that he feels for his other friends. He asks himself whether, perhaps, racial antagonism accounts for this mutual strangeness; but he must reply in the negative. In the depth of his heart there are stronger bonds uniting him with Heinrich Bermann and Leo Golowsky than with his non-Jewish companions, or even with his brother. Yet, if this is so, why is he ill at ease when he listens to Heinrich and Leo discussing the Jewish question? To his own surprise, he discovers that he himself had been guilty of unjustified animosity toward the members of the Jewish race—an animosity that he could not explain on the basis of personal experience. He, too, had light-heartedly contributed his share towards swelling the distrust and defiance which he encountered among Jews. "This thought aroused in him a growing discomfort, which he could not quite interpret, and which was nothing else than a vague recognition that pure relations could not flourish, even between individually pure characters, in an atmosphere of folly, injustice, and insincerity." Until this atmosphere is completely dissipated, many centuries will pass. Meanwhile each Jew will have to find his own way out of despair and disgust, his own way to a freedom that will permit him to breathe unmolested. "Perhaps there are really some who will have to go on to Jerusalem," says Schnitzler, through the mask of Heinrich Bermann. "I fear, however, that, on reaching this illusory goal, they will find themselves in a still greater mess. I do not believe at all that such wanderings on to freedom can be undertaken *en masse* . . . for the roads to freedom do not run through the lands out yonder, but rather through our inner selves. It is up to each person to find his inner path. To do so, it is, of course, necessary for him to attain clarity within himself, to light up the most hidden corners of his soul, to have the courage of following his own nature, and not to let himself be led astray. Yes, the daily prayer of every decent person ought to be: no straying from the inner path!"

Der Weg ins Freie is Schnitzler's confession of faith. It is the faith of a skeptic. Yet, just because Schnitzler is an extreme skeptic, he even doubts his own doubts. Just because he is so logical, he soon sees the limitations of logic. Just because he wants to motivate every event minutely, he realizes early in his work that rational motives alone never really explain any event. Recognizing the insufficiency of reason, he does not throw it overboard but still advocates it as a guide which can light us part of our way. But beyond reason, he asks us to probe within the depths of our being and to follow the dictates of our own nature. This inner voice will lead us, more surely than any set dogmas, on to the road of freedom.

CHAPTER XI

THE ROAD TO FREEDOM

THERE is only one health, but there are many sicknesses; and each sickness must follow its own course, and requires its own specific cure. There is only one moral code in each society—the moral code approved by that fictitious personality called the average man. Deviation from this code is called immorality, and there are many types of immorality. All, however, have this element in common: they burden the human conscience with a sense of sin and guilt. They thus prevent the individual from breathing freely, and from enjoying to the fullest extent the beautiful panorama of life that unfolds itself to unclouded eyes. Though Schnitzler, the determinist, recognizes that we must all bow to necessity, he does not interpret necessity as including every moral whim of society; he does not ask us to submit willingly to the accepted doctrines of the day, which the majority imposes in the form of written and unwritten laws. He, instead, holds that a person enters on the road to freedom only when he follows the dictates of his own personality irrespective of moral taboos or social ostracism. Freedom is, to Schnitzler, that ideal state in which a person understands himself and the world about him. No person can enter on the road to freedom so long as he lies to himself, nor so long as he feels conscience-stricken when others condemn those actions of his which he deems justified.

Since each individual is unique, each situation in which

an individual finds himself is also unique. It may, therefore, happen that a person, after mature thought, will regard it as his duty not to do what all others assume that it is his duty to do. Thus, to take an extreme example, a young man may lead an honest girl astray and give her a child. The general reaction would be that it is his duty to marry her. Yet, marriage might be the worst possible solution for both; and the young man might rightly feel that it is his duty to desert her. He would be acting immorally, if, against his better judgment, he were to yield to public opinion. He must build his own life. He must base his decisions on the laws of his own nature.

Der Weg ins Freie derives its main plot from this situation. Baron Georg von Wergenthin, twenty-seven years old, drifts into an affair with Anna Rosner, a kind, respectable, middle-class girl. On the day on which she gives birth to their child, he leaves her. In doing so, he is aware that, though others might be blamed for acting thus in similar situations, no guilt is attaching itself to him. He is certain that he is behaving correctly.

The beginning of the novel goes back to the last decade of the nineteenth century. Early in this decade Schnitzler published the drama entitled *Das Märchen*. In this he concentrated on the fate of Fanny Theren, a young girl whom society has unjustly condemned as a fallen woman, because she has loved with her whole being and has been deserted by the man to whom she gave herself. Schnitzler in this thesis-drama withheld all sympathy from Friedrich Witte, the seducer. Friedrich is the unpardonable villain who has brought dishonor to the girl who trusted him, and who now informs her smilingly of his coming marriage to someone else. Friedrich, the man, might remain the untarnished hero in the eyes of all his acquaintances; Fanny, the woman, might suffer severe reproaches even from the idealist Fedor Denner; to the dramatist, however, Friedrich's attitude was easy to understand, and Fanny's action was more pardonable than the action of myriads of women who marry for a home.

Upon completing this play, Schnitzler was hailed as the continuator of Ibsen and applauded for his vigorous attack upon vicious moral prejudices. The very approval with which the play met caused the physician and casuist to doubt the trustworthiness of his conclusions. He asked himself whether there were not, also, situations in which a seducer, such as Friedrich Witte, deserved, not condemnation, but rather commendation for bringing about a girl's so-called "downfall."

In *Liebelei*, the play published immediately after *Das Märchen*, he touched upon such a possibility. When Weiring is praised for saving his sister from dangerous experiences, he replies sadly that, though he formerly took pride in his role as guardian of her morals, he is no longer convinced that he was justified in depriving her of such experiences. "I still see her before me, as she often sat opposite me in the evening, near the lamp, in this very room, and looked at me with her quiet smile, with a certain resignation—as though she wanted to thank me for something; and I—I would have preferred to throw myself on my knees before her, and to beg her pardon for saving her so carefully from all danger—and from all joy."

An entire play, in which the seducer was to be presented almost in the guise of a benefactor, was outlined by Schnitzler in the nineties. It was to consist of three acts and was to be entitled *Die Entrüsteten*. The first act was to depict the depressive atmosphere of a bourgeois home: Father and mother are morose. The daughter is pale, sickly, hysterical. She gets nothing out of life. An elderly gentleman would be willing to marry her, but the doctor advises against such a marriage. The mother, or a relative, tells her that she could live as she pleased after the wedding. The daughter, nevertheless, refuses to take the old man. The second act was to show the girl cured of her hysteria and flushed with health. Everyone is happy, until the discovery is made that she has a lover. The family is horrified. Her rascally brother promises to compel the lover to marry her. In the third act, the seducer was to defend himself with the claim that he saved the girl and imbued her with joy. She, too, was to justify the affair. In answer to her mother's chiding, she asks: "Why should I, the poor girl whom no one will ever marry, be condemned to eternal chastity?" She insists upon respect from her lover, even from her second lover. When the latter, in spite of all his affection, hints at his magnanimity in pardoning her for her past, she counters: "How about my pardoning you?"

In this brief outline, we can see vaguely fore-shadowed the entire Rosner family of *Der Weg ins Freie*: father, mother, Josef, and Anna. We can also recognize in the charming seducer the prototype of Georg von Wergenthin, who at this stage was conceived in the likeness of Anatol, the aesthetic epicurean.

In two outlines of 1897 this character is further developed. He is a musical dilettante, a composer who has not the patience nor the willpower to complete any work of importance, an orchestral conductor who is not very keen about accepting appointments. In his passive, unheroic fashion he drifts light-heartedly into an affair with Anna.

She finds in him, for the first time, ecstasy, romance, and escape from the sordid monotony of her parental home. Before long, however, the intoxication of the love experience subsides. Both face the difficult question of their future adjustment. Would marriage be the proper solution? If not, what is likely to be the effect of their temporary affair upon their remaining years?

In *Märchen*, Schnitzler had demonstrated how laden with unpleasant consequences such an affair could be for the woman, while it left the man unseared. In *Liebelei* he had again stressed the tragic results that might ensue from an experience which the man considers purely as a flirtation, but which the woman must atone for bitterly. Christine Weiring and Fritz Lobheimer can be regarded as the forebears of Anna Rosner and Georg von Wergenthin. A bullet put an end to Fritz before his affair with Christine had passed its peak. Suppose, however, that Fritz had lived on. What would likely have been the later course of his love affair?

In the outlines of *Die Entrüsteten*, Schnitzler pursues the relations of such a pair from this point on. In accordance with his usual dramatic technique, he assigns the hero, Georg von Wergenthin, who resembles such aesthetic epicureans as Anatol and Fritz Lobheimer, a contrasting friend, Heinrich Bermann, the skeptical realist. Similarly, the serious heroine, Anna Rosner, who may be regarded as the successor of Christine Weiring, is assigned a frivolous companion in Else Ehrenberg.

In a dialogue between the two women, outlined by the author in 1897, Else congratulates Anna upon her splendid fortune in having acquired a lover; while Anna, taking a different view of the matter, weeps bitterly at such a sad lot. Schnitzler includes in the same outline a conversation between the two men, in which he seeks to make clear that a wedding would be a very imperfect way out of the difficulties in which the young man thoughtlessly placed the trusting girl. If, on the one hand, Georg's first step in entering into intimate relations with Anna was immoral, because she did not have the makings of a coquette, then, on the other hand, his plan to rectify his error by marrying her would be equally unfortunate, because she was not by nature fit to be the mate of an unstable epicurean. Instead of atoning, Georg would merely be bringing lifelong unhappiness upon Anna and himself.

From 1897 until the close of 1900, Schnitzler wrestled with this drama. Each additional outline accentuated the difficulty of the central problem and rendered the relations between the various characters more complex. On July 6, 1900, he made his last attempt to arrange his material within the framework of five acts. On the basis of this elaborate outline, he began the actual writing of the first act on October 10, 1900. Immediately, however, he realized the impossibility of continuing. He wrote: *"Als Stück kaum möglich, als Roman zu entwerfen."* From 1900 until the summer of 1902, he was engaged in repeatedly recasting his material into the mould of a prose epic. On August 9, 1902, five years after he conceived the original plan, he was finally able to write the first page of *Der Weg ins Freie*. It was a proud day for Schnitzler. It was the very day on which his son Heinrich was born. The five years of planning for the novel were followed by five years of actual writing. During the last three years he devoted his main efforts especially to this work. In November, 1907, he could at last put the finishing touches on the creative work of a decade.

The novel offers a cross section of the pre-war Viennese society that Schnitzler knew best: men and women of the lower aristocracy and the upper middle class; salon heroes who are removed from the daily struggle for bread; and beautiful heroines who are troubled solely by problems of love, even though they might dabble at times in art or politics.

Georg von Wergenthin, the outstanding character, has spent a melancholy summer in Vienna. The death of his father has left him lonely and confused. His irresponsible roaming and his philandering are drawing to a close. At twenty-seven, he must make up his mind to pursue a definite calling. The study of law, which he carried on as long as his father was alive, has failed to satisfy him. He has a decided preference for a musical career. Yet, though his few compositions arouse general interest, he does little to develop his talent. He likes to dream of a future full of work, fame, and love; but he does not care to exert himself unduly. A position as orchestral conductor is offered to him. Perhaps he ought to accept it. Meanwhile, however, his attention is diverted in another direction. He has made the acquaintance of Anna Rosner, a young lady who wants to go on the stage but who has had to content herself with giving music lessons, because her voice is not suitable for theater performance. Georg likes to play duets with Anna. He is charmed by her simplicity, and attracted by her kindness and purity. Before long the two find themselves under the spell of mutual love. They make no attempt to resist each other. Within a month Anna is wholly his. Sometime later she confides to him that she is expecting a child. Georg immediately fears possible complications, and he yearns to regain his carefree mood. He has the unpleasant task of breaking the news to her parents. He has to put up with gentle reproaches on all sides. Even the sympathetic physician, in whom he confides, does not regard the matter lightly. To avoid a scandal, the lovers travel to Italy. Weeks of undisturbed bliss follow. Anna assumes that Georg will marry her. He himself has toyed with the idea, though he never mentions it. There are moments when he feels tempted by other women, and there are moments when he feels that Anna alone can make him supremely happy. The months pass without his having to make up his mind. Finally, Anna gives birth to a stillborn child. Georg almost condemns himself as a murderer, for he did not really desire the child. At the same time, he experiences a certain relief. A telegram from the theater at Detmold brings him an offer of a position as orchestral conductor. When he returns to Vienna after six weeks at Detmold, Anna has recovered from her experience and has resumed her music lessons. He suggests that they might leave town together for a few days, and she replies gently that she would not like to go through their experience a second time. Georg realizes that this is the moment to calm her fears by promising to marry her. "He sensed how she was waiting for this word with a hope whose fulfillment she herself no longer really believed in. But he remained silent. If he had said what she longed to hear, then he would have bound himself anew; and now he realized, as never before, that he wanted to be free. Still she rested on his knees, her cheek leaning on his cheek; they were quiet for a long time, knowing that this was the end."

Georg departs without remorse. He accepts the interpretation of the experience that Heinrich Bermann gives him: "Anna was, perhaps, fashioned to be your beloved, but not your wife. Who knows but what the person she will marry some day, will not have every reason to be grateful to you, if only husbands were not so terribly stupid!" With this moral absolution from his best friend, Georg leaves the city of his youth; and, in a mild intoxication of pain and freedom, he sets out on the road toward his new center of activity.

Heinrich Bermann is left behind. The profoundest thinker among Schnitzler's young men, he is, also, the unhappiest, perhaps because he probes too deeply. Wanting to understand everything, he is at the same time aware that understanding exercises no appreciable influence upon our emotions, and rarely affects our actions. Like Falkenir, in *Komödie der Verführung*, he is almost ready to curse his gift of understanding. An experience, such as the one which Georg could so lightly toss from his conscience, would probably have filled Heinrich with relentless remorse. An affair with an actress brought him almost to the verge of insanity. Of this affair, Heinrich remarks: "Somewhere in my soul, I felt myself without guilt. And elsewhere, perhaps deeper in my soul, I felt myself guilty . . . and still deeper again, guiltless. It all depends upon how deeply we peer into ourselves. And if the lights on every story of our soul were lit up, we would find ourselves at one, and the same, moment guilty and innocent, cowardly and heroic, foolish and wise." Depth of insight does not lead to clarity, but rather it leads to a realization of the abysmal confusion within us. It does not make for happiness, but rather for a knowledge of our helplessness. It does not simplify our lives, but rather renders us aware of the infinite, uncontrollable threads that determine our acts.

A person afflicted with insight, can never take refuge in lines of conduct mapped out by others. He has no firm foundation under his feet, as have his uncritical neighbors who subscribe to the tenets of an established party or religion. For him there are neither precedents nor preconceived judgments. Every day he must discover anew the world and himself. In every person and every relation, in every thought and every deed, he sees some element that is unique, and that requires a new interpretation. Every experience brings him face to face with a different problem. In such an unstable world, fiction may take on the semblance of truth, and truth become fiction; murder may prove an act of kindness, and a kindly deed lead to murder; a seducer may emerge as a benefactor, and a saintly wife may be a destructive power.

Does Schnitzler, then, wish to pave the way for moral anarchy by negating existing moral assumptions? Does he, by his merciless arraignment of conventional ethics, aim to undermine the pillars of family life and social institutions? Does he, by opening our eyes to infinite possibilities and by tearing down all taboos, also lend his approval to everything we may undertake, to every piece of villainy and every form of excess? Not at all! Schnitzler is not immoral, as his foes assert. On the contrary, he profoundly believes that every one of us has in his breast a moral seismograph that registers every minute deviation from the right path. In some mysterious way we know at every moment what we may or may not do. We even know when we may commit murder without sinning. But we also know that many of our acts for which we receive praise, are not necessarily good. Our chief moral fault lies in our not listening to the infallible measuring instrument in our souls, in our not trying to understand ourselves, in our seeking to ferret out justifiable motives for everything we do whether rightly or wrongly. The only criminals for whom there is no atonement are, according to Schnitzler, those who act against their own nature. The only duties, the fulfillment of which may, perhaps, at times benefit others, are the duties one owes to oneself. All moral confusion results from the fact that but few people know their own true nature, and that only a very small minority of these have the courage to act in accordance with it. Yet, these alone are on the road to freedom.

CHAPTER XII

THE CURSE OF UNDERSTANDING

THE road to freedom is the road of understanding—a road that can be trodden only by those individuals who liberate themselves from social prejudices and preconceived morals, a road that must be discovered separately by each person as he makes an intensive study of his own unique nature, a road upon which it requires considerable courage to set out and upon which few continue for more than a brief interval.

Though, at first sight, freedom and understanding may appear to be the ideals or guides of conduct set up by Schnitzler in *Der Weg ins Freie*, a further study of the works of the Viennese thinker reveals that he does not countenance an overdose of either. He rather holds that an excessive amount of freedom leads to a disintegration of one's personality, and that understanding, if carried too far, acts as a paralyzing force.

Too much freedom and too much understanding wreck the marital happiness of Cäcilie and Amadeus, in *Zwischenspiel*; of Dionysia and Erasmus, in *Die Hirtenflöte*, and of Aurelie and Falkenir, in *Komödie der Verführung*. In the end these characters recognize that direful results might have been averted, if freedom had been curbed by responsibilities, and if understanding had been overridden by passion. Falkenir reaches the point even of cursing his gift of insight, and voluntarily atones with his life for his error in urging upon his beloved an excess of freedom.

Falkenir is the successor of Stefan von Sala. Both noblemen are aging widowers, melancholy and philosophic, tolerant and kind, widely traveled and much experienced. For a last time, youth and love come to them. Sala is almost apologetic in accepting Johanna's proposal, for he well knows that he cannot fulfill all of a young girl's dreams. He even assures her that she need not consider herself bound to him for all time. Falkenir shrinks back when his proposal is accepted by Aurelie. After due deliberation he realizes that, as a man of forty, he had no right to ask a girl of twenty-two for her hand. Her very acceptance is, to him, merely another proof of her inexperience. He fears that her choice was dictated not by love but by friendship and trusting admiration, especially since his rivals were two younger men: the handsome prince Arduin of Perosa, and the world-famous poet Ambros Doehl. In vain does Aurelie try to calm his misgivings. Foresight and caution impel him to refuse the woman he has wooed. He can hear the rushing of eternal streams, the dark eternal streams that flow uninterruptedly from man to woman, and from woman to man. Never will he feel safe in possessing her, and he does not want to expose her and himself to repeated scenes of jealousy. His hair is turning gray, while she is confronted with an inexhaustible wealth of experiences from which to choose. If her training has wrongly taught her that she must confine her choice to one man, and if she does prefer him to Arduin and Ambros, he does not intend to take advantage of her error. In her dancing he can see her body twisting and turning, and her soul expanding and floating on to infinite possibilities. All doors are open to her, and she is responsible to no one. Let her, therefore, be true to her nature and follow every lure. He will always remain her friend. If ever she is in need of him, she has merely to call on him. But to unite their diverging destinies in marriage would be a crime which he could not justify.

Falkenir's attitude and his hasty departure leave Aurelie confused and hurt. In a welter of wounded pride and passionate intoxication, she yields to the blandishments of the first seducer who crosses her path, Max von Reisenberg, and becomes his mistress. The artist Gysar paints her portrait, but his effort is unsatisfactory. Only when the model gives herself to him, does he succeed in producing a masterpiece. Aurelie, disgusted and attracted by this strange overture, is about to ask Gysar to leave, but suddenly changes her mind. Gysar is her second lover. He paints her in the nude. When she first sees herself in this portrait, she strikes the artist in the face and calls him a liar. Yet, she soon has to acknowledge that her image in the painting is a truer expression of her real self than is the mask with which God provided her and which she normally carries exposed to every gaze.

She seeks refuge in loneliness from this real self that she discovered in the midst of a sensual orgie. The poet Ambros, who remains her sincere friend throughout these questionable adventures, brings her to Gilleleije, a small village on the Danish coast, in which she is to regain her health and composure. Here she again encounters Falkenir. Aware of his guilt in exposing her to temptation, he wishes to save her from gliding still further into the unknown. She, however, denies him the right to interfere. She not only absolves him from all guilt, but she even goes so far as to thank him for having showed her the road predestined for her, the road she has trod. As the first person to recognize her true being, he deserves, in her eyes, the title of benefactor. Falkenir confesses that it is all too easy to satisfy himself merely with this insight. Beyond all insight begins that something which gives meaning to all human relations—that something we call responsibility—and Falkenir is ready to assume his share thereof. This new wisdom he brings with him from the loneliness of a hundred days and nights, and he calls it love. He, therefore, no longer hesitates to offer to Aurelie security, refuge, and his name. Now that unsafe times are coming and war clouds are gathering, he wants her to have in him a person whose protection she can, without hesitation, invoke in every situation. If, in his folly and pride, he once scorned happiness, simply because its permanence was not guaranteed by fate, he has now become chastened and more modest. Aurelie reminds him that remote possibilities conjured up by his imagination, affected him so deeply that they sufficed to make him flee from her. How, then, will he be able to face the realities of her past? His reply is: "Possibilities are more sinister ghosts than realities that are past. In myriad shapes, and nameless, they float about us; as wishes and dreams, they sit down, like uninvited guests, at our table and drink the elixir of life from our cups, while we, athirst, watch them with our dry, hot lips . . . Experiences, no matter how horrible, belong to the past. In the light of day, of our day, Aurelie, the ghosts of the past are wafted away, and become as naught."

Aurelie calls upon Falkenir to translate this theory into practice. If he has the courage of his new convictions, then let him face the ghosts of her past. Yet, though Falkenir seems to come through the ordeal almost unscathed, Aurelie is still not convinced that a common happiness can ever be in store for them. "There still flow, Falkenir, through my heart, untamed, the eternal streams to which you opened my ear. The glare of torches, the sound of flutes and violins, the rushing of waves at night, a flattering voice, the fragrance of lilacs—and your Aurelie glides into the arms of a seducer, of a friend, of a stranger who knows how to take advantage of the hour . And if I vowed to be faithful to you—and even if I could—do the eternal streams flow no more? And do you today believe that I could ever belong to you as completely as you think you must require me to? Or that you could ever possess me as entirely as no man ever possessed a woman; or woman, a man; or any human being, another—and as no one ever should?" Falkenir answers these questions with the words: "No, Aurelie, I do not hold such a belief, now less than ever. On the other hand, I no longer maintain that it is the meaning of love to rejoice in the security of one's possession. To love means to fear, to struggle, to woo. To love means to have to win ever anew the object of one's desire; to be ready to renounce, if fate thus decrees, and to be a home, a lasting home, for the beloved from whatever distance she may come and into whatever distance she may long to go." Aurelie, whose faith in love is, however, shattered beyond repair, sees only one sure way of keeping their relations untarnished and of avoiding future infidelities; namely, the way of death. She, therefore, takes Falkenir down with her to a watery grave. "For a second both heads were above the water. It looked as if they kissed each other. And the countess still smiled. Neither he nor she stretched out an arm; and suddenly both sank together, with incredible speed, as though the sea had swallowed them."

This tale of Falkenir and Aurelie, which forms the central theme of *Komödie der Verführung* (1924), bears such striking resemblance to *Die Hirtenflöte* (1911), the tale of

Erasmus and Dionysia, that in spite of the thirteen years' difference in the dates of their publications, one is inclined to conjecture that both works must have had a common source or background. A study of Schnitzler's manuscripts yields the interesting fact that both tales owe their origin to the year 1908, the year after the completion of *Der Weg ins Freie.* Erasmus was the prototype of Falkenir, and Dionysia of Aurelie. It is very probable that Schnitzler for a time wavered between a dramatic and a narrative cloak for his fable. He made outlines for both. From March 22 until April 12, 1908, he even wrote out in detail the first act of the dramatic version. In this act, Falkenir was to tell Aurelie the story of the aging stargazer, the husband of a young wife who knew nothing of her possibilities until her husband urged her to follow the lure of the shepherd's flute. Aurelie was to reply that she, in such a situation, would never follow the tone of the flute, and Falkenir was to counter with the remark that her motive would be fear of life and that she was seeking in him a bulwark against the eternal forces active within her.

Before proceeding beyond the first act, however, Schnitzler who had a habit of working on several themes at the same time, undertook in June, 1908, to convert his *Frieberg-Novelle,* of 1902, into a tragi-comedy, which, as we have seen in a preceding chapter, afterwards appeared under the title *Das weite Land.* To Friedrich Hofreiter, the aging hero of this tragi-comedy, were transferred many of the traits of Falkenir. Friedrich, too, was chosen by a young girl, Erna Wahl, who preferred him to more youthful suitors; and he, also, refused her, after at first encouraging her. His refusal, too, was based on the opinion that she must have erred in her choice because of her inexperience, that she really belonged to youth, and that he did not want to live with her in perpetual insecurity and inevitable jealousy. The inclusion of the "Friedrich Hofreiter—Erna Wahl" episodes in the play *Das weite Land*, therefore, for a time precluded the completion of another play with similar characters, the same situation, and the identical conclusions. The temporary scrapping of the "Falkenir-Aurelie" dramatic fragment left Schnitzler free to issue as a separate work the romantic legend of Erasmus and Dionysia, which he formerly intended to embody in briefer form in the first act. This work appeared in 1911 as *Die Hirtenflöte*.

Not until 1918 did Schnitzler revert to his rejected dramatic fragment, and then only because he could not dispense with Aurelie and Falkenir as important figures in a play, *Der Verführer*, with which he had occupied himself for decades, and which he had not been able to bring to a satisfactory close. This play centered about a charming seducer, at first called Friedrich von Rosenberg and afterwards renamed Max von Reisenberg. For this frivolous young man, who seduced three girls and who emerged smiling from his experiences, with his faith in himself unimpaired, Schnitzler had sought as a counterpart a woman who also underwent three love adventures but who, as a result, emerged broken in body and soul, having lost all faith in herself and others. In Aurelie, Schnitzler had found this person. In Falkenir, he had had a mouthpiece through whom he could voice his own painful insight. The episode of Aurelie and her three suitors had been skillfully grafted on the plot of *Der Verführer* by making her one of the three girls seduced by Max von Reisenberg.

In this shape, *Der Verführer* had come to bear close resemblance to Schnitzler's earliest drama, *Das Märchen*

(1891). One might almost have mistaken it for a later edition of this drama with Max, the seducer, in the role of Friedrich Witte; Aurelie, the so-called fallen woman, in that of Fanny Theren; and Falkenir, the prospective husband, in that of Fedor Denner. Fedor's theory that women with a past were preferable to their respectable sisters who married primarily for the comfort of a home, had been merely carried to its logical conclusion by Falkenir's view that women who had gone through various love adventures made better wives than those who had never gone outside the bounds of conventional morality and who, therefore, dwelt constantly in a murky mist of unfulfilled wishes. The breakdown of Fedor's theory when subjected to a practical test, because this theory failed to take into account the peculiar structure of male psychology, had found its parallel in the case of Falkenir, when Aurelie questioned his ability to banish from his mind the ghosts of her past.

An examination of Schnitzler's manuscripts leads to the interesting discovery that the first outline of *Der Verführer* actually does go back to Schnitzler's earliest period; that the first references to this play do date from the years when Schnitzler was at work on *Das Märchen;* and that the original hero, Friedrich von Rosenberg, alias Max von Reisenberg, was really conceived in the image of Anatol, the dramatist's favorite character at the close of the 1880's.

The first fragmentary concept, which may have been jotted down as early as 1888, has the following content: "'Come in, Nelly, do come in. Sit down near me, permit me to tell you that I love you. Experience a last romance before you hurl yourself into the life of a coquette, a life in which you will degenerate.' And she experiences the last romance, the last night. At the gray of dawn he leaves

Ostende; in the evening she sells herself. Dialogue: (How he finally implores her!) 'Don't do it! I will make you happy.' 'No, no, I can't lose any time.' The preceding evening she had already told him that she was to be with this person, and that . . . "

This fragmentary note contains in embryonic form one of the main episodes of *Komödie der Verführung*, the episode between Judith Asrael and Max von Reisenberg. This episode is developed in great detail in an unpublished narrative entitled *Der Verführer*. The hero, Friedrich von Rosenberg, meets a Viennese acquaintance on board a steamer that has just sailed from Hamburg. In the midnight hours he relates to this fellow passenger a most unusual experience that made him suddenly depart from Ostende, a Belgian resort at which he had expected to spend several weeks. While looking out from the terrace of his hotel in that city, he had seen a girl pass by whom he knew from a casual acquaintance three years before. At that time, while in Ischl, he had joined an excursion group of which she was a member. During the walk Judith had confided to him her family history. She had neither father nor mother, and was living with her sister, who had married a wealthy but unattractive banker, and who betrayed her husband by having affairs with handsome cavalry officers. "I myself won't marry," Judith added. "I intend to become a coquette . . . I really don't understand my sister. Why all this fear and secrecy? . . . I feel that I could not be faithful to any man, that I should like to live free and amidst plenty, and that I don't want to betray anybody. Well, then, I would rather become soon what I must become eventually. Of course, there is still time. For another year I'll probably stay at home and study singing. But that is only for the sake of appearances. I have no desire to sing in public at concerts, or to go on the stage. Besides, I have no talent, and I am very lazy. You see, the only thing left for me is to become a coquette." Friedrich von Rosenberg treated as a jest these apparently childish words spoken by a seventeen-year-old girl whom he had met at the home of a respectable family. Yet, when he recognized her three years later at Ostende, she recalled to him their conversation and told him that she was about ready to enter on her chosen career. She seemed amazed at his incredulity. She felt that there was nothing unusual in her action, except, perhaps, the frankness with which she discussed it. She interpreted her meeting with him at the very beginning of her career as a favorable omen, and she foresaw coming triumphs. That night she experienced in the arms of Friedrich the first bliss of womanhood; and on the following morning, in spite of his unsolicited vows of faithfulness, she made him promise to leave and not to recognize her if he ever encountered her again. He remained until evening, hoping that she might change her mind. But when he saw her disappear from the ballroom, arm-in-arm with an American millionaire, he was so overcome with disappointed longing and so consumed with pain that he departed with utmost speed and took the first boat out of Hamburg.

The frivolous, and yet melancholy, tale of the seducer and the coquette is linked by Schnitzler in a fragment of October 9, 1904, to two other tales of seduction centering about the same hero. The underlying thought of this fragment is that we use the word "seduction" to cover a multitude of experiences which may be worlds apart. As a proof of the variety of relations designated by this single expression, the hero tells of three different affairs through which he himself has passed. All three may be called seductions; and yet, one experience was humorous, another sentimental, and the third tragic.

Soon it occurred to Schnitzler that these three successive experiences could be combined into a single play if he would have the hero meet the three girls for the first time at a masquerade ball on the same summer evening, while the air was saturated with longing and flirtations. The dramatist, thereupon, rearranged his material in a new outline under the title *Der Verführer und die drei Jungfrauen.* The circle in which the play was to revolve was that of *Der Weg ins Freie.* Of the three women, one is easily recognizable as Judith, the incipient coquette. Another is cast in the likeness of Anna Rosner. After the hero's affair with her, he flees because he fears permanent entanglement. Sometime later he discovers that she expects a child. He feels he must marry her, but she tells him it is unnecessary. She is proud of her motherhood, and will herself care for the child. The third girl bears the marks of Heinrich Bermann's actress, who committed suicide. When the report of her tragic end reaches the hero, he replies that nothing has really changed for him. He is without remorse, since their affair was at an end and she was far away from him.

With the completion of *Der Weg ins Freie* in 1907, and with the transferring of the main traits of the second heroine to Anna Rosner, and of the third heroine to the actress, there remained but scanty material for the play of seduction. Schnitzler attempted in a version of March, 1908, to substitute Aurelie for the actress; but, as we have seen, he never got beyond the first act, for at that time he determined to abandon the entire play. This decision enabled him to execute further raids upon the discarded material. The seducer who alternates between three women was utilized in the comedy *Die Schwestern*, a comedy first outlined in 1908 and 1909; then written in prose as a one-act play in 1915, with Casanova substituted for Max von Reisenberg; and finally completed in verse as a three-act play in 1918.

Not until the end of the World War and the collapse of the Austro-Hungarian Empire did Schnitzler regain interest in the discarded fragment, *Der Verführer*. The light affairs of the beautiful heroines and the melancholy heroes lost their trivial aspect when viewed as the expression of an overrefined culture that has passed its zenith. The eager grasping of every sensation, no matter how trifling, was seen as the nervous reaction of a civilization that was skeptical of its survival—as the convulsions of a patrician class that knew its days to be numbered.

By projecting the action of the play into the critical day of August 1, 1914, the dramatist sought to produce the same effect of impending doom that he had achieved in his play *Der Schleier der Beatrice*. In this effort he was not successful. The European catastrophe of 1914 and the Viennese comedy of seductions called forth entirely different emotional responses, and could not be forged into a unity. The necessity of introducing additional characters complicated the action still further. Besides, the three types of seductions failed to merge satisfactorily in the artist's mental laboratory. Judith, the coquette, retained much of her burlesque origin; Seraphine, the sentimental violinist with the maternal complex, lacked the breath of life; Aurelie alone held the center of interest. In spite of years of experimenting with various episodes and characters, Schnitzler could point with pride only to the "Falkenir-Aurelie" scenes. These he invested with the charming tenderness and the mellow wisdom of his old age. These alone justified the publication, in 1924, of *Komödie der Verführung*.

CHAPTER XIII

DREAM AND REALITY

THE apparent contradictions often encountered in Schnitzler's works, result from his anxiety to view each problem from various angles. As the infinite possibilities encased in every situation are unlocked, the sharp distinctions between truth and fiction, reality and illusion, give way. The world becomes surcharged with magic, and our daily scenes take on a semblance of fairyland. A fragrant mist, a glamorous veil, overhangs all objects. We see of one another only our silhouettes, our shadows.

Schnitzler's characters range from prosaic Philistines, who, like the armorsmith Cyprian, are never troubled by metaphysical questions, to extreme skeptics, whose confusion of dreams and reality borders on the insane. The latter include Andreas Ungnad, in *Der Gang zum Weiher* (1926), and Robert, the hero of *Flucht in die Finsternis* (1931). Ungnad takes refuge from his doubts in the philosophy of solipsism: "If I close my eyes, all light is extinguished. If I hold my breath, no flower exhales fragrance. If I fall asleep, the world sinks in slumber. And if I die, the world dies with me." Robert succumbs to "persecution-mania," since he finds no certainty anywhere on earth and can, therefore, trust nobody.

As early as 1897, Schnitzler attempted, in the one-act play *Paracelsus*, a blending of illusion and reality. In the following year, he again presented, in *Der grüne Kakadu*, truth and fiction inextricably intertwined.

Der grüne Kakadu is the name of an inn in Paris on the eve of the French Revolution. The innkeeper, Prospère, is a former theater director, who hates aristocrats but who, nevertheless, earns his living by amusing them as best he can. His impoverished actors appear evenings in his tavern disguised as cutthroats, and they tickle with gruesome tales of crime the tired nerves of the decadent nobles who seek piquant sensations. But, acting and living, pretending and being, are not always kept apart. On the one hand, the player who practices inflammatory orations before his select audience finds himself suddenly confronted with hungry masses whom he incites to storm the Bastille; while, on the other hand, the murderer who has just completed his prison sentence applies for a dramatic role in which he can play what he has really experienced.

Prospère's chief attraction is the leading actor Henri. Having married his madly loved Léocadie, Henri intends to leave Paris and to settle peacefully in the country with this beautiful harlot, who will henceforth tread the path of virtue. On the eve of July 14, 1789, he appears for the last time and tries to display his best talent by performing a scene of jealousy. He tells excitedly of coming unexpectedly upon his newly wedded wife and the Duke of Cadignan, and of murdering this aristocratic wretch. From the horrified expressions on the faces of his colleagues, Henri discovers that his wife really has betrayed him, and that everybody believes his story of the Duke's assassination. This fiction turns to truth a moment later when the Duke enters, and Henri now stabs him in earnest. As the Duke falls, shouts are heard outside. The mob has just stormed the Bastille and is marching past with the head of Delaunay. The noblemen, who imagine that the whole scene was prearranged in order to win their applause, suddenly find themselves facing real, and not imaginary, danger. The confusion of play and reality is a favorite device in Schnitzler's mature works. Konrad Herbot, in *Die grosse Szene* (1915), cannot emancipate himself from his roles. "Love, treachery, murder—all this, though it really happens, weighs no more in his eyes than it might if it were part of his dramatic lines." In *Fink und Fliederbusch* (1917), a journalist writes, under the name "Fink," reactionary articles in an aristocratic weekly, and, under the name "Fliederbusch," liberal articles in a democratic daily. Engaging in a fierce controversy with himself—a controversy which leads to a duel with himself—he is finally asked by both parties to state his true position. He replies: "The day before yesterday I was Fliederbusch; yesterday I was Fink; today I am both, or perhaps, neither."

Schnitzler often expresses the opinion that the illusion conjured up by an artist may contain more truth than actual facts that were or will be. Memory fails us; hope deceives us; mystery envelops us. Every night we descend into a strange realm in which our dreams exercise a more tyrannical sway over us than does all the wealth or logic of dazzling daylight.

In *Traumnovelle*, Schnitzler depicts dream hours that blend so perfectly with waking hours that the reader is unaware when the former begin and when the latter end. This tale, which appeared in 1926, centers about a couple who resemble Amadeus and Cäcilie, of the drama *Zwischenspiel*. The Viennese physician Fridolin and his wife, Albertine, have attended a masquerade ball. The insignificant flirtations which brushed past them at this affair pursue them in their dreams. The suppressed desires and "extra-marital" longings of both seek expression in illicit visions, when the rational faculties are dulled.

On the evening after the ball, a contemplative mood comes over the tired couple. Conscious of the dangerous adventures that might have resulted if they had followed every stirring of the heart, they confess to each other the ebb and flow of their inexplicable emotions. Albertine recalls a summer day at a Danish resort when she was seized by a violent affection for a strange young man. On that day she would have been ready, at a moment's notice, to leave her husband and child. But the young man paid not the slightest attention to her, and so she remained a faithful wife. Fridolin, too, tells of a similar temptation that once crossed his path. The confessions of the couple are interrupted by the maid. The physician is asked to hasten to the bedside of a patient who has just suffered a stroke.

Fridolin now goes through a series of weird experiences. He finds the patient dead. When he comforts the surviving daughter she confesses her long concealed love for him; and in the presence of the corpse she folds him in her arms. Disturbed by the arrival of her betrothed, Fridolin leaves. A prostitute invites him to follow her. A former classmate, who has been reduced to earning a living by playing the piano at disreputable coffeehouses, enables him to make his way into a secret night club, at which masked, naked women dance with elegant gentlemen of high society. Fridolin is warned by a beautiful mask to escape; but he remains, and is detected as an intruder. In his extreme peril, he is saved by the mysterious woman, who ransoms him with her body. He arrives home at four in the morning, and finds Albertine asleep. As he watches her, she awakens with an hysterical laugh. She, too, has gone through exciting adventures.

She felt herself in the arms of many men and dreamed that her husband insisted upon remaining faithful to her even when subjected to torture and condemned to death. That Fridolin should submit for her sake to suffering and crucifixion at the very time when she was betraying him with others seemed so silly to her that she could not refrain from laughing shrilly, and thus she awoke.

Fridolin is horrified. His wife's dream reveals her true nature to be faithless, cruel, and treacherous. He determines to avenge himself by continuing his adventures of the preceding hours. But these adventures now afford him little satisfaction. The daughter of the deceased patient arouses no longings in him. The prostitute has been transferred to the hospital. The mysterious woman is nowhere to be found. She may, or may not, be the suicide whose body has been delivered to the morgue. He returns again to the side of his wife, and, sobbing, confesses his aberrations. "What are we to do now, Albertine?" he asks. She smiles, and after a moment's hesitation replies: "It seems to me we ought to be grateful to fate that we have come through unharmed from all adventures—from the real and the imaginary ones. "Are you so sure of this?" he asks. And she answers: "As sure as I am of my belief that the reality of a night, or even of a person's entire life, does not wholly represent his innermost truth. "And no dream is wholly a dream," she adds, with a sigh.

Clouds appear and overshadow human relations. Clouds burst, and lightning flashes. Then the sun reappears, and all is calm again. Why place greater weight upon actual happenings that are over than upon dream phenomena that flit past? We live but one of many possible lives. We know little of the whims of the "world will"; we cannot even foresee our own whims, if whims they be and not necessities preordained since the beginning of time. A sultry summer day, a glowing autumn night, a winter's ball, a spring's excursion wrest reasoning human creatures out of calm pleasures and sorrows, and hurl them into dangerous experiences. From these experiences they may either awaken, as from a dream, and return to their accustomed ways, or they may be transformed in body and soul. After employing the latter ending in many serious works, Schnitzler chooses the former alternative for his drama *Im Spiel der Sommerlüfte*, the last drama to be published during his lifetime.

Though the play did not appear until 1930, the first idea for it goes back to 1892. The atmosphere of the closing nineteenth century is unmistakable. The sculptor Friedlein and his wife, Josefa, occupy a summer house at Kirchau, a village not far from Vienna. The husband generally comes out only during weekends. He is a successful artist; he is optimistic and tolerant, unconventional in his manners and unfettered in his morals. He sees in his respectable wife merely the woman, a person who has freed him from certain unpleasant features of bachelordom. She has always been faithful to him; and, without giving the matter much thought, he takes it for granted that she will always continue to be so. Josefa feels rather neglected, even though she has a famous husband and a seventeen-year-old son. She is only thirty-six, and desires still tremble within her—desires that are not satisfied by her family. "No mother holds her son and no wife her husband as she would like to hold them. When a call or a lure resounds from somewhere, they rush out into the storm, into the night, into life, and she remains alone."

Her niece, Gusti Pflegner, is the lure that comes to her lively boy, Eduard, and makes him forsake his botanical studies for a more dangerous enthusiasm. Gusti is practically engaged to a Viennese physician, Dr. Faber. She is recovering her health in Josefa's country house before entering upon a theatrical career at Innsbruck. In Schnitzler's original outline of 1892, the youth, who plays with a revolver, is, in a fit of jealous rage, to shoot her betrothed. Since this theme was, however, afterwards treated by Max Halbe in the well-known drama *Jugend* (1893), a less tragic development suggested itself. Young Eduard, inflamed by Gusti's presence under the same roof, forces himself upon her on every possible occasion. On the last day of her stay, they are both overcome by the sultriness of the evening in the open; and, without making any serious effort at resistance, they yield to the temptation of the moment. Gusti is delighted by the freshness and naturalness of the boy in contrast to the premature seriousness of her betrothed, the physician. For Eduard she signifies the first experience of manhood.

The summer night also weaves magical bonds between Eduard's mother and the young chaplain of the resort. This priest, conscious of his mission as the intermediary between God and man, is profoundly shocked to discover within himself certain desires which he has been taught to classify as human failings. A peculiar relation develops between him and Josefa. She brings him down to earth; and he leads her into higher, hitherto unsuspected regions, where duty and renunciation dwell.

The magnetic currents circulating between Eduard and Gusti, and between Josefa and the chaplain, reach their climax of intensity with the outbreak of a hurricane. When the storm subsides, there follows a temporary reaction in the form of remorse. There is a general feeling that something tremendous has happened which will completely transform the entire future of the people concerned. A few hours later, however, when the sculptor and the physician return from Vienna and the usual atmosphere again prevails, then the importance of the night's tempestuous experiences gradually recedes. Each person goes back to his essential interests. Eduard resumes his botanizing; the priest, his reading of the mass; Gusti, her acting; the physician, his hospital practice; the sculptor, his art; and Josefa, her devotion to her husband. A late summer night's dream has come and gone. Nothing has really happened.

If only we could realize how relatively unimportant at bottom are these playful relations which we dignify with such tragic names as infidelity and seduction! If only all of us would acknowledge jealousy to be ridiculous, hate to be unwarranted, and vengeance to be absurd! In *Stunde des Erkennens*, a one-act play begun in 1901 and published in 1915, a husband waits maliciously ten full years for his hour of revenge, in which he might punish and debase his wife, because he imagines that she has betrayed him with his successful professional rival. When the long anticipated hour arrives, this revenge turns out to be meaningless and unnecessary, since his suspicions have been wrongly directed. For ten years he has lived amidst a nightmare of illusions, while his wife has done her utmost to make him happy.

If Schnitzler's men, generally, lay greater stress upon fidelity than do his women, the true explanation of this tendency is male vanity and hurt pride more often than love. This view is stressed in the comedy *Die Schwestern oder*

Casanova in Spa. The original outline, jotted down on March 22, 1908, has the following plot: "A person is very jealous. He wants to kill his wife and her lover. Then he learns that the lover does not know who his beloved is, and that the woman, in turn, has assumed that her lover is someone else, a person who in reality died on the day following the husband's discovery of the situation. To depict: how the husband's jealousy disappears, and how he comes to the realization that it is only vanity and the fear of appearing ridiculous which have nearly caused him to become a murderer. The lover himself relates his adventure to the husband. The latter thereby discovers that the former was unaware of his beloved's identity."

This plot was developed in a detailed outline on September 11, 1909. A one-act prose version was completed in 1915. In this version Schnitzler substituted for the nameless lover a semihistorical personage, young Casanova. The final poetic version in three acts appeared in 1919. The charming hero, famed for his amatory exploits, makes his way at night into the wrong room, and unwittingly enjoys delights that were meant for the girl's betrothed, while the woman who expects him waits in vain throughout the endless hours of the night. On the following day the girl tells her beloved of the night's experience. She feels that in reality nothing has happened, that she has not been unfaithful at all, that she has merely drifted about on the wave of a dream. "When I awoke in the gray of dawn, I was alone. I lay with open eyes and well knew that the experience of this night would have appeared, not only to others, but even to myself a few hours ago, as abysmal guilt—not just guilt towards you, Andrea. And yet, my soul was light and gay. Astonishment rather than horror filled me at the observation: Only yesterday I was so wholly wrapped up in you that the thought of another man's touching my hand with impure designs filled me with disgust; and this morning I awakened from the wildest embraces of a stranger as free from remorse as one awakens from childlike slumber! What was inconceivable only yesterday had become an actual fact today! And yet, I feel myself to be the very same person that I was, unchanged and unconfused." Andrea, the man, rages and storms. He will have nothing more to do with her. Then he learns from Casanova that this adventurer had no idea whom he held in his arms. Immediately Andrea's anger vanishes. He is willing to forgive magnanimously, and to regard the episode as merely a dream. But now his fiancée refuses to treat the matter lightly, and Casanova is called upon to pass judgment.

The adventurer's decision, tinged with Schnitzler's usual skepticism and mild melancholy, effects a reconciliation of the estranged couple. He asks them not to expect too much of each other, and they will thus avoid disappointments. The human soul is doomed to eternal wandering and eternal restlessness. Hence, no person can ever be a lasting home for another. At best, he can be but a temporary haven to which the beloved may return from time to time in order to recuperate from tiring excursions. Let no man, therefore, assume that his beloved is faithful, even when she resists temptation by seeking refuge in his arms; for he really does not know of whom she may be dreaming while she is in his arms. Let him not put too much trust even in her most sacred oaths, for she may reason that God is sparing in the use of his lightning strokes. And even if she kills herself in order to eradicate, by this sacrifice, his last doubts of her love, she may be hoping in her heart of hearts that she will reappear as a blessed spirit to gloat over his tears of remorse. Only a woman's voluntary return to her mate or her beloved can be accepted as true love or fidelity, and that, too, but for a brief space of time.

The more often Schnitzler analyzes abstract words, such as "love" or "faith," "truth" or "freedom," the less certain are we of their exact meaning. Each concept is divided into its component parts, and each component is resolved into its minute elements, and each element is still further subdivided into its manifold possibilities. In the end, we do not know whether we are dealing with the ultimate essence of reality or with figments of the imagination; and Schnitzler uses all the art at his disposal to further this confusion. It is his intention to break down the boundaries that we have erected between reality and fiction, truth and illusion, waking life and dream life, necessity and freedom, earnestness and play, good and evil, love and hate. He would substitute for them a constant awareness of the relativity of all knowledge and experience, a deep distrust of all dogmas, and a solemn awe before the insoluble mystery of all creation.

CHAPTER XIV

THE MELODY OF RESIGNATION

IN the seventy-second year of an eventful life, surrounded by the plaudits of an entire generation, Henrik Ibsen writes his epilogue, *When We Dead Awaken;* and in this dramatic masterpiece he laments the fact that fame is but the vanity of vanities, and that no final wreath of glory can ever compensate sufficiently for preceding renunciations and privations. In the last decade of a contemplative career, with the shadows of age and loneliness growing ever more sinister, Arthur Schnitzler, the continuator of Ibsen, writes his epilogue, *Der Gang zum Weiher;* and in dramatic verses he gives utterance to his deep disillusionment with art as a substitute for active life, and to his sad recognition of the fact that fame is not in itself an end worth striving for. The themes that interested the Viennese thinker from his earliest youth pass once more in review before him, and for the last time he pronounces judgment upon the figures that haunted his imagination for a third of a century. The call of life that first rang out so magnificently in *Der Schleier der Beatrice,* that reached its height of intensity in *Der Ruf des Lebens,* and that lured so bewitchingly in *Komödie der Verführung,* now resounds sweetly and intimately before it fades away forever.

Heine once declaimed against the foolish superstition that fame warmed the poet's grave, and he assured his readers that a far better warmth was given by an infatuated milkmaid, who kissed with thick lips and smelled of dung.

Merely to live, to breathe, to pant on earth, seemed to him more thrilling than to rule as lord of the underworld. Similarly Schnitzler, in the mask of the poet Sylvester Thorn, voices his conviction that immortality is a fairy tale which, like other fairy tales, can delight us only as long as we listen with living ears. A person who has not been sated with experience will gladly exchange the pale, magic drink of eternity for a single pure ray of sunlight, for a single breath of earthly air. He will gladly sell the ecstatic singing of a thousand angelic choirs for a single human sound. The touch of a friend's hand, a May morning, a cup of wine, a melody, the fragrance of a flower, the glance of a faithful dog—the many trifles that we hardly notice as long as we dwell in the realm of light outweigh by far the tears of unceasing lamentation which trickle into an unfeeling, mute grave. They mean far more than the golden inscription on the marble tomb beneath which the body of the eulogized deceased rots; far more than immortality, the lie of lies; far more than the deepest gratitude of coming worlds; far more than the fervent understanding of generations still unborn.

Sylvester Thorn, who utters these opinions, is the successor of Filippo Loschi, of Heinrich Bermann, and of Falkenir. Tired of restless roaming, he returns after an absence of ten years to the castle of Mayenau. Here he is being awaited by Baron Albrecht, an ex-chancellor, who devotes his leisure hours to the dictation of his memoirs, and by the baron's daughter Leonilda, who remembers the poet as the radiant ideal of her girlhood. Unable to stave off any longer the inroads of age, Sylvester wants to marry the singer Alberta—his sweetheart of former years, who has again come back to him and who is about to become a mother—and to establish a home for his declining days. But when he meets Leonilda, and when this maturing maiden mistakes her adoration of the poet for genuine passion, he is once more dazzled by an illusion of love, the will-o'-the-wisp he has pursued throughout his life; and he impetuously asks her father for her hand. The baron warns him against taking such a rash step: youth and age cannot long be happy together. Without denying the truth of this admonition, Sylvester feels, like all other aging Schnitzler heroes, that the joy of love, no matter how temporary, is sufficient compensation for whatever unpleasantness might follow. Leonilda means to him what Johanna Wegrat does to Stefan von Sala; Erna Wahl, to Friedrich Hofreiter; and Hilda Wangel, to Ibsen's Master Solness: the last defense against old age. Sylvester, therefore, leaves in order to put an end to his affair with Alberta. Thirty-six hours later he is back at Mayenau, having meanwhile witnessed the death of Alberta, after she had given birth to a stillborn babe. Not at all disconcerted by this tragic event, he again woos Leonilda. He still lives on, and holds that no amount of mourning will help the dead. The fewer the years remaining to him, the more precious they become. To live means not to renounce, but to struggle for, every bit of joy. Leonilda is now, however, beyond his reach. Youth, in the figure of Konrad von Ursenbeck, the active son of a martial father, has arrived to claim her; and she has learned to distinguish between the call of the blood and admiration for a great artist. "It would be a poor world, if youth were everything," remarks Sylvester, when he hears of Leonilda's new infatuation, that has begun during his absence. Her father, who urges him to give up the vain struggle against a younger rival, replies: "Youth means so much that, were you to place on one side of the scale, held by the maiden, fame and power and wisdom, and on another side the blond down about a stripling's lips, the latter would by far outweigh the former." Sylvester trusts in his experience to win again the girl whom he had succeeded in impressing once before. But all his eloquence is in vain. He must bow to the inevitable—to old age, to loneliness.

For a quarter of a century Schnitzler shrank before the specter of advancing age. Love, war, and even death, he was willing to accept as adventures. Age alone was pitiless fate, against which one was utterly helpless. Julian Fichtner was the first of Schnitzler's long list of characters who struggled vainly to retain their hold on fast-ebbing youth. Friedrich Hofreiter put a bullet through the young man who called upon him to make way for the rising generation, and yet he finally had to accede to this demand. Casanova, at sixty, exerted all his skill and cunning to win triumphs which in earlier days would have been his almost without effort, and in the end he had to confess shudderingly that time had, also, taken its toll of him. Dr. Gräsler and Falkenir retired from the arena of battling interests when they had barely passed the zenith of their lives; and Sylvester Thorn, with all his genius, proved no match for rash and self-confident youth.

In *Der Gang zum Weiher*, Konrad von Ursenbeck is Schnitzler's symbol for youth, the new youth that thinks less intensely than did its elders and that, therefore, acts more vigorously. According to Konrad, the world is poisoned by the breath of its graybeards. "One should kill them all; otherwise, respect, cunningly taught to youth and ingrained in its marrow, will soon make it as weak and cowardly as its elders." Eager for action, Konrad is sent by the military party with an important message to Baron Mayenau. He urges upon this ex-chancellor the necessity of bringing to bear upon the ruler immediate strong pressure in favor of war. He has no patience with hesitant and cautious diplomacy. He speaks for the army, that wants to strike quickly and to invade the neighboring land before effective resistance can be offered. The baron, who, at this critical hour, has again been called to the chancellorship, decides, however, to exert all his statesmanship in behalf of peace. Before setting out for the capital to take up his duties, he makes Konrad promise not to leave Mayenau until he returns. He does this, partly in order to keep the young firebrand from the army, and partly in order to bring him into closer contact with Leonilda and thus prevent her falling a prey to Sylvester's overtures. When the chancellor hastens back to Mayenau, after having patched up a temporary peace, he finds Konrad and Leonilda mates before God. The young man has, meanwhile, become aware of the chancellor's intention to detain him at the castle, even by the magic power of love if necessary. As a result, he prepares to flee. The chancellor, incensed at the youth's irresponsible behavior, wants to compel him to marry his daughter. But Leonilda refuses. She will not let anyone decree her behavior, or determine her future for her. She insists on Konrad's being set free. At this moment a courier arrives to announce the beginning of hostilities. While efforts for peace were under way, the first battle had already begun. Therefore the course of events could no longer be arrested. At one stroke everything takes on a different appearance. Konrad exults at the prospect of action and fame. The chancellor gives up his pacific office and takes command of his old regiment on the battlefield. Sylvester Thorn, out of place in this new topsy-turvy world in which all he holds dear is tumbling about him, goes off to commit suicide. He alone steers clear of the frenzy of patriotism and the hysteria of war. He alone cannot get excited about his fatherland. His home is in the disputed province that changes hands every few decades, and he has learned to differentiate between the intimate concept of home and the more remote fiction of a fatherland. If Konrad is Schnitzler's symbol for the active young man, the type acclaimed by the Expressionistic generation of the war and post-war period, then Leonilda is the symbol for the young girl of today and tomorrow. She no longer has to wage a stubborn fight against society for her every bit of freedom and joy, as did her predecessors in the preceding decades. The problem of the fallen woman—a problem that faced Fanny Theren, the heroine of *Märchen*, in 1891—is nonexistent for her. Though she has given herself to Konrad without the blessings of either Church or State, she is not weighed down by remorse, nor does she feel herself inextricably bound to him. On the contrary, she maintains that neither of them is under any obligation to the other, certainly not under the obligation to remain faithful for even a single hour. "Did I make you lord over myself in that moment when we glided enchanted into each other's arms? Did I give you my yesterday and my tomorrow along with my today? Moreover, are you sure it was really myself that I gave you? . . . Now, first, you will have to woo. The nymph was yours. If you want the wife, you will not win her with the insolence of youth. And unless you watch out, the nymph will again descend to the depths, just as she rose from them." Leonilda is, thus, a passionate advocate of absolute freedom. Her conscience is the only tribunal that she recognizes. She even refuses to be engaged to Konrad before he leaves for the front, because she does not want to bear fetters of any kind nor to impose any upon him. She does not want to restrict her liberty of act, thought, or emotion; and she can give no guarantee for the state of her affections when he returns from battle. In her frankness and lack of sentimentality, she goes beyond Johanna Wegrat and Erna Wahl, two of her prototypes whom she resembles in many details.

Leonilda is Schnitzler's ideal because she is true to herself. Remorse cannot assail her, because she resolutely conforms to the laws of her personality. Society may pronounce its harsh judgment upon her conduct, but she will not quail. She has inner fullness. She is on the road to freedom. She will, of course, pay the price that all of Schnitzler's men and women pay who insist on preserving their individuality intact—the price of loneliness. She will, perhaps, pay it somewhat earlier in life than others, for she cannot wholly forget herself even in the intoxication of first love, and she is not likely ever, thereafter, to embrace the illusion that young people delight in—the illusion that absolute communion and understanding between human beings is a possibility.

The aging Schnitzler shudders at the loneliness enveloping every one of us. "There are many types of loneliness that are more pure, more painful, and more profound than the types we normally designate by this term. Has it ever happened to you that, after you enjoyed yourself in a large group, all the people present suddenly appeared to you as ghosts, while you yourself were the only real being among them? Or, have you never in the midst of a stimulating conversation with your friend become conscious of the absolute meaninglessness of all your words, and of the hopelessness of your ever understanding one another? Or, have you never rested blissfully in the arms of your beloved, and then suddenly discovered, by unmistakable signs, that behind her forehead were flashing thoughts of which you had not the slightest suspicion?"

Conversation comes to have merely an atmospheric value to the later Schnitzler, since he holds that, after a certain maturity, there is really nothing vital which one person can possibly communicate to another. He himself in the last years of his life speaks and writes for the pure joy of the activity itself, knowing full well the absurdity of all efforts to convince his auditors or to modify their actions. The extreme skeptic keeps aloof from the conflict of interests that rages in contemporary Europe. The preacher of tolerance withdraws from a world of growing intolerance. The internationalist looks askance at the resurgence of a virulent nationalism. The kind physician shakes his head ominously as he recognizes the feverish symptoms of hate that threaten to overwhelm entire countries. The literary master flees from the disagreeable post-war atmosphere. He transposes to preceding centuries the scenes of his last works. He writes, not for his generation, but for one that is to come. "I speak to those who are to come. They alone are my friends. What disturbs you is that I am still alive. You are right. Our sojourn on earth falsities our true being. Our life is a mask that clings to us. But when this mask is torn down, then whatever remains exists, not for us any longer, but only for you."

With the collapse of the dual monarchy and the ascendancy of a new youth, Schnitzler came to be regarded as an historical rather than as a contemporary figure. He was upbraided for his indifference to the economic plight of the present day. He replied that, while the bread-and-butter question was undeniably important, yet it was only after it was out of the way that the really eternal problems began. Charged with never having offered a definite solution to any of these, he countered with the suggestion that the eternal problems would not be eternal if he could solve them once and for all. The accusation was hurled against him that his range was very narrow, and his subjects unimportant. He met this accusation with the calm answer that perhaps he must plead guilty, but that he really did not know of any themes which were wider or more important than the call of life, the dance of death, the lure of love, and the facing of fate.

Schnitzler, the artist, may have had at his command no more than these four strings: life, death, love, and fate but these sufficed. Like a master violinist, he could evoke from them more varied and more subtle melodies than could others who played on instruments with a greater number of strings. Of these four themes he fashioned an atmosphere of his own, and compelled us to submit to its lure. At the mention of his name there comes over us a nostalgia for youth and the play of love, for carefree days and frivolous nights. There arise before us scenes in Vienna and along the banks of the Danube, in Meran and Bologna, in Spa and Gilleleje—all wrapped in the colorful haze of adventures. There crowd about us figures and faces, from sentimental Anatol to dashing young Casanova, from sweet Mizzi to noble Leonilda; and yet, we need but to put forth our hand to touch theirs, and they will retreat from us into their more glamorous abode in fairyland. For their real home is not among us. Though for a time we may be attracted by their kindly smile, by their passive nipping of pleasures, we ultimately must ask ourselves whether the fascination of their world is not really a subtle poison that acts upon our dynamic will, sapping us of all strength and courage. Amidst the snorting of machines, the dizzy whirl of the modern metropolis, and the harsh clash of conflicting interests, of what importance are their subtle questionings and their impotent resignation, their tired negations and their skeptical affirmations? Why, we ask, do they never stake their all to win all? Why do they never burn their bridges behind them, and strike out with full force? Why are they forever hesitant? Why don't they *act*?

We are about to condemn Schnitzler, when it occurs to us that these questions might also be asked of Shakespeare's Hamlet. They might be asked of most of Turgenev's heroes. Schnitzler's characters are, indeed, weak-willed Hamlet's. They are "Turgenev" types. But is their weakness wholly a vice? May not their failure to act be justified on the ground that they understand too much, and understanding paralyzes action? Just because they do see so clearly the possibility of their opponent's view, their weapon is lowered before it can strike, and their hate yields to sympathy. Kindness and sophistication characterize most of Schnitzler's figures. They characterize the author himself, the product of an ancient and overrefined culture.

Schnitzler sang the swan song of old Vienna. He caught in his gentle hand the last golden glow of its setting glory, and converted it into art. Two cities symbolize today German hope and German despair, German will-to-power and German consciousness of doom and decline. They are Berlin and Vienna, the robust capital of Prussia and the charming metropolis on the Danube. Berlin is the rational, practical center—a city that will not acknowledge defeat. Vienna is the city of dreams—a city of mild sweetness, of music and dance tinged with sadness; a city with a glorious past and a less glorious present; a city which was once the aristocratic center of a vast empire, and which is now the impoverished capital of an impoverished country. Berlin has tremendous vitality. It aims to be the New York of Europe. Vienna accepts defeat as its lot. It accepts it with a sad jest and a certain charming melancholy. The peculiar culture and aroma of this city are present in Schnitzler's works, as they are in the songs of Franz Schubert and the waltzes of Johann Strauss. Though the Viennese physician is dead, his dramatic and narrative melodies will long continue to haunt our ears, and to make their way even to our very heart of hearts.

AFTERWORD

REMEMBERING ARTHUR SCHNITZLER

M Y first meeting with Schnitzler took place on 25 July 1929 and my last meeting on 25 August, 1930. It was Richard Beer-Hofmann who initiated my earliest visit to Schnitzler. I had been acquainted with his works ever since Camillo von Klenze, my German teacher at the City College of New York, assigned to me in the Spring Semester 1919 as a class assignment the translation into English of Schnitzler's narrative *Das neue Lied* (1905). Thereafter, I read most of Schnitzler's plays and short stories and taught several of them to my students of the 1920s.

During my summer vacations of that decade, I sought to make the acquaintance of German writers whose works I was teaching or intended to teach, so that my teaching would not be based solely on book knowledge. During the summer of 1929, I arranged to meet Ricarda Huch and Arnold Zweig in Berlin and then to proceed to Prague before attending the World Zionist Congress in Switzerland. En route from Prague, I decided to stop over in Vienna, a city in which I did not know a single person. I did, however, have a letter of recommendation from Supreme Court Justice Louis D. Brandeis to Ottilie Franzos, the widow of Karl Emil Franzos, whose most important novel *Der Pojaz* I had undertaken to translate.

I arrived in Vienna toward the end of the day of Hugo von Hofmannsthal's death. When the cab driver at the road station asked to what hotel he was to drive me, I recalled that the Hotel Sacher was mentioned in Schnitzler's *Anatol.* If it still existed forty years after the publication of the playlets, I would make it my resting place for the one day I intended to stay in Vienna. As events turned out, I spent the rest of the summer there.

On the following morning, I paid a visit to Ottilie Franzos. She appreciated my interest in her husband, who had died a quarter of a century earlier and whose posthumous fame was receding.

In the afternoon I paid a condolence visit to Anna Kellner, whose husband, the Shakespearean scholar, Professor Leon Kellner, had recently passed away. I told her of his kind comments on my first book *Shelley in Germany,* when it appeared in 1924. She was deeply moved and suggested that I meet Beer-Hofmann while in Vienna.

When I did meet him on the following afternoon, I led the conversation to the Viennese writers I knew best: Schnitzler, Hofmannsthal and Stefan Zweig. Hofmannsthal had just passed away and Zweig was in Salzburg. Schnitzler, however, was living in Beer-Hofmann's vicinity and he arranged for my meeting him.

During our meeting on the afternoon of 25 July, Schnitzler was a gracious host and immediately put me at ease. He listened attentively and stimulated me to do most of the talking. I later discovered that his intense listening was due to his difficulty in hearing rather than to anything unusual in my discourse.

He opened the conversation with a routine, innocuous question as to whether this was my first visit to Vienna. I replied that I had been in Vienna in December 1922 but had not stayed in this historic city for more than a few hours.

Why only for a few hours?

I hesitated before answering frankly. I knew that he loved Vienna with all his heart and soul and I had been with him only a few minutes. However, his kind yet piercing eyes dispelled all hesitation. I told him that I had arrived on a Sunday afternoon and found placards with the words "Juden 'raus!" I dined at the Ratskeller but could not leave it because a demonstration of anti-Semitic students was taking place outside of the building, while in the large Rathaus chamber a meeting of Jewish protesters against anti-Semitism was being harangued by Councilman Robert Stricker and other Jewish speakers of various parties. After the speeches, the audience was escorted under the protection of a Jewish self-defense group for several blocks, constantly harassed by youngsters shouting vituperative slogans, until it was safe to disband. I was caught up in the escorted group and felt humiliated. I left for Venice in the evening and for seven years I did not want to return to a city where anti-Semitism was rife.

Schnitzler listened to my narrative and commented that, if I were to avoid cities and lands having anti-Semites in their midst, I would have to avoid many places of interest and cultural importance. After all, anti-Semitism was not a Jewish problem. It was a Jewish misfortune but a problem for non-Jews who had to reconcile their ideal beliefs and their love for mankind with their hatred and discrimination against their fellow men of Jewish origin. I told him that I was aware of his treatment of this theme before the World War in his novel *Der Weg ins Freie* and in his drama *Professor Bernhardi*. Our conversation then veered to these two works. He mentioned that Otto Brahm did not believe that the play would be successful on the stage. Schnitzler tried to convince Brahm that he was wrong. "Ein Drama wirkt, weil die Charaktere leben. Professor Bernhardi lebt. Er ist mein Vater. Und diese Szenen sind wahr. Auch *Der Weg ins Freie* ist zum großen Teil persönliches Erlebnis. Auch die Charaktere sind echt. Nur daß ich die Schlamperei Gottes etwas verbesserte. " Our conversation then turned to other literary themes. I told Schnitzler that of all his plays *Der einsame Weg* meant most to me, and that I regarded the scene between Johanna and Stefan von Sala at the opening of the fourth act as among the finest of dramatic dialogues. He told me that he too was fond of the play. "Die Szene im vierten Akt ist mir auch die liebste. Sie gefällt mir auch viel besser als die Vater-Sohn Szenen. Sala ist lebendig. Als ich das Drama schrieb, habe ich noch lange mit ihm gesprochen. Man wollte in ihm Hugo von Hofmannsthal sehen. Ich sagte: 'Hugo, ich habe deine schrecklichen Eigenschaften abgezeichnet.' Aber die Figur ist doch erfunden." Sala was conjured up by Schnitzler as a composite portrait of persons he knew but not of any specific individual.

Our conversation shifted to other Austrian writers. Schnitzler called my attention to Adalbert Stifter, whom he greatly admired. He was surprised that I had never read this fine Bohemian novelist who excelled in descriptions of nature's gentler moods. Though Stifter during his lifetime did not have many readers, his vogue would increase and he would remain a literary classic. To veil my insufficient knowledge of Austrian writers, I reverted to conversing about his own works.

I mentioned that in my teaching I contrasted the love triangles in his works with those in Hauptmann's works. I pointed out that Hauptmann generally dealt with the man between two women, one of whom was his wife and approximately his own age, while the other was the dream-girl. While the man aged in play after play from *Einsame Menschen* to *Vor Sonnenuntergang,* the girl remained eternally young and alluring. On the other hand, Schnitzler's dramatic triangles centered about the problem of the woman between two men, one of them her husband and most often older and the other an Anatol-Casanova-Don Juan type. Schnitzler smiled and commented somewhat roguishly: The man between two women, is that a problem? He will find a way to have both. The woman between husband and alluring lover—ah—that is indeed a problem. For a woman to leave husband and children and to risk social opprobrium and the loss of economic security in order to follow the call of passion necessitates difficult psychological adjustments.

Between my first and second meeting with Schnitzler, an event occurred that changed my entire life. On 27 July, two days after my afternoon at his home, I took my first walk with the Viennese young lady who was to become my life's companion. It was my twenty-eighth birthday and our walk from the Cobenzl to the Kahlenberg and through the Vienna Woods lasted a full day. On the following afternoon, I asked her parents for her hand, after having obtained her consent. When I again visited Schnitzler, I asked him to be a witness to my wedding. Beer-Hofmann was the other witness. They were the two Viennese writers I had come to admire most and who knew me best. Both agreed. Schnitzler came with his son Heinrich to the Seitenstetter Temple, where the wedding ceremony was performed by Chief Rabbi Feuchtwang. He signed the marriage certificate with his Hebrew name: Aaron Schnitzler. After the wedding, Schnitzler left for his vacation at St. Moritz, and I did not see him again until the following summer.

Before returning for the Fall Semester in the United States, I spent much time with Beer-Hofmann, who for the next decade and a half until his death in 1945 exerted a great influence upon my thinking. I also found time to become acquainted with the two talented Viennese poets, Ernst Waldinger and Uriel Birnbaum.

During the academic year 1929-1930, I wrote my essay on Beer-Hofmann which appeared in two issues of the *Monatshefte für deutschen Unterricht* and which was expanded into a book, published in 1936.

My summer of 1930 was devoted to gathering material at Schnitzler's home for a book which was to appear for his seventieth birthday in 1932. I was interested in ferreting out his attitude toward basic, so-called eternal problems, such as the call of life, the dance of death, the lure of love and the facing of fate. This I could do best by a *Leitmotiv* analysis of his published works, discovering common denominators or approaches amidst many variations. But I was also interested in learning how he had arrived at his conclusions, how his mind worked as he delved ever deeper into the intricacies of the human psyche. This I could best discover by studying the genesis of his works from his original, primitive concept, through his various outlines and changing versions down the years until the final published text.

I would visit Schnitzler on afternoons, rarely mornings. On each occasion I would ask him for his files on a single major play that interested me most. I began with my favorite play, *Der einsame Weg,* and continued with *Zwischenspiel, Der Ruf des Lebens, Das weite Land, Professor Bernhardi,* and *Der Gang zum Weiher.* I would take each file to my hotel, work through the material and return the file to him a day or two later, when he would answer my questions on items that were not clear to me. On taking leave, I would depart with a new file. These sessions lasted from 28 June to 25 August, interrupted by his vacation with his son Heinrich at St. Moritz in July. On 26 August he left for a vacation in Marienbad and I returned to New York. It was my intention to be back in Vienna for the summer of 1931 to complete my research in his archive. On my final visit, he had given me an insight into the almost inexhaustible richness of his archive. He showed me a play that he had begun in his fourteenth year. He spoke to me of a play he hoped to complete before long, to be entitled "Der Zug der Schatten." He told me that though several decades had passed since he first conceived the theme of the play, *Der Ruf des Lebens,* and a quarter of a century since its publication, he was still dissatisfied with its conclusion. He still wanted to change the final act and was contemplating various alternatives.

We spoke of his *Komödie der Verführung.* I mentioned that, while he was vacationing in the Alps, I was spending a week at Gilleleje, a village on the Danish seacoast of which I had never heard until I read this play. It was there that Falkenir had his last meeting with Aurelia before both walked down from the only hotel and into the sea that covered them. Schnitzler's files had revealed to me that he had wrestled with the seduction themes of the play since 1888 and with the Falkenir-Aurelia scenes since 1908, although this comedy with a tragic ending was not published until 1924. He had long wavered whether to use the plot for a narrative or a drama. Finally, he incorporated the plot in both genres. In the short tale *Die Hirtenflöte* of 1911, he

portrayed the aging star-gazer Erasmus and his young wife
Dionysia as the central figures, but they continued to haunt
his imagination until he refined the theme and reintroduced
these characters as the aging Falkenir and the alluring
Aurelia in his comedy of seduction. Nevertheless, he was
not sure that their suicide in the sea was the proper ending
of the dilemma in which they found themselves.

At my taking final leave of Schnitzler in 1930, I expressed the hope that I might return a year later in order
to continue my examination of the files he had just shown
me. As he accompanied me to the front door, I muttered
the usual conventional phrase "Auf Wiedersehen." His last
words, as he stood under the lamp, hanging above the door,
were "wenn ich noch lebe!" These words were characteristic
of him, since premonitions of death accompanied him
throughout his adult life.

As Stefan Zweig told me when I visited him in Salzburg
about a week later: "Schnitzler dichtete aus Todesangst und
Lebenssehnsucht. Er war eigentlich niemals ein Lebemann,
aber er beneidete seine Freunde, die es waren und die Vor-
bilder für die Anatol-Figuren waren."

I corresponded with Schnitzler until his death on 21
October 1931. His letters to me have been printed in the
volume of *Briefe 1913-1931* (S. Fischer Verlag, 1984).
When I sent him an advance copy of my articles on the
genesis of three of his plays, he replied on 13 May 1931:
"Ihre Artikel über die Genesis des *Einsamen Wegs*, über
das *Weite Land* und über den *Bernhardi* habe ich gern
gelesen, ich finde sie vorzüglich geschrieben, aufschlußreich
sogar für reich und geradezu amüsant. Ich hoffe mit der Zeit
durch Sie noch mancherlei über mich und meine Werke zu
erfahren."

When I completed in the fall of 1931 my essay on "The Call of Death and the Lure of Love—A Study in Schnitzler," I sent him a copy but, alas, it no longer reached him. I completed my book before the end of the year. It was published by Prentice-Hall for his seventieth birthday in 1932, but he was no longer among the living. I dedicated the book to Richard Beer-Hofmann, his lifelong friend, who understood him best among the literary galaxy of *Jungwien* and who had initiated our first meeting.

When I sent a copy of the book to Stefan Zweig, he replied: "Ich habe mit großem Vergnügen Ihr Buch erhalten, das durch seinen uns immer noch schmerzlichen Tod eine tragische Aktualität gewonnen hat; ich glaube nicht, daß der Nachlaß irgend etwas enthält (außer den Tagebüchern), was das runde und vollkommene Bild, das Sie geben, wesentlich erweitern würde, und so hoffe ich, daß Ihr Buch nicht nur das erste englische über Schnitzler sein, sondern auch dauern wird. Ich bin nicht sehr patriotisch, aber mich bewegt ein Gefühl besonderer Dankbarkeit gegen Sie, daß Sie diesen Mann, den ich stolz meinen Freund nennen durfte und der Österreich vor der Welt repräsentiert, so lebendig und liebevoll dargestellt haben. Ich will überall, wo ich Gelegenheit finde, auf dieses Ihr besonderes Buch hinweisen."

Jerusalem,   Sol Liptzin
14 September, 1990